Brothers In Arms

Jordan Wheeler

Fourth Printing August 1997

All characters in this novel are fictional and any resemblance to any person, living or dead, is purely coincidental.

Pemmican Publications Inc. gratefully acknowledges the assistance accorded to its publishing program by the Manitoba Arts Council and Canada Council.

Printed and Bound in Canada - Hignell Printing Ltd.

Canadian Cataloguing in Publication Data

Wheeler, Jordan, 1964-
  Brothers in arms

Contents: Hearse in snow. -- Red waves. -- Exposure.
  ISBN: 0-921827-07-5

I. Title.
PS8595.H445B7 1989   C813'.54   C89-098115-9
  PR9199.3.W544B7 1989

**Pemmican
Publications
Inc.**

Unit 2-1635 Burrows Avenue / Winnipeg, Manitoba / Canada R2X 0T1

Acknowledgements:

Foolscrow and Byron Gislason for musical support; Wayne Tefs, my old hockey coach, for his brilliant editing; Paul Chartrand for a bit of reality; Wayne Courchene for his bad jokes; Charles Cowley Pratt; The Callahans for their friendship and the odd meal; Rick Rennpferd for his positive skepticism; Spiderworks for their antics; PTAM for their employment; Mike Foster; Rick Zastre and the Rat Pack; Blair Cooley; Tim Cruly; Albert McLeod; The Courchene In-Laws; Maria Campbell; George Clutesi; The Pratt Clan; Dr. Clay Dyck; TSN; The People of Clyde River, NWT; the Kematch brothers; and my cat, Midnight.

Special Acknowledgements:

To Winona Stevenson my sister, Theresa Stevenson my niece, Tammy McLeod my other sister; Bernelda Wheeler my mom for having me, Pete Wheeler my dad for my conception; and to my family, Tanis my partner, Cameron my son, and Kaya my daughter for all their support and inspiration.

In Memory of:

Hearse In Snow   Colin Pratt

Red Waves   Buddy Wolf, Anna Mae Aquash,
and all the others

Exposure   Paul P.

"I shall see our young braves and our chiefs sitting in the houses of law and government, ruling and being ruled by the knowledge and freedom of our great land. So shall we shatter the barriers of our isolation. So shall the next hundred years be the greatest in the proud history of our tribes and nations."

-Kanentakeron, *Touch The Earth*
(Chief Dan George)
1899-1981

HEARSE IN SNOW

It is a dark, February night. Paul Dieter and Charlie are plowing through the deep snow in the northeast corner of the Berens Landing Reserve. Nearly half the reserve knows Charlie, a lazy animal but an affectionate one. His devotion to Harry Cochrane has earned him respect. 'A good dog,' he's called, 'but ugly.'

The moon, in its third quarter, spreads a bluish hue on the land. The wind is calm and the air is crisp. The stars, dwindled by the moon, still shine their brilliance.

About thirty feet ahead, Charlie stops on the windward side of a small hill. Paul stops fifteen feet away. From here he can see the lights of his parents' house. To the south, skidoo headlights cross the frozen surface of Berens Lake. Charlie is sniffing in the snow, his long, hairless tail wagging intensely. Paul feels uneasy. The windward side of the hill is in shadows, but a snow covered lump bulges beside the dog.

When Paul advances, he finds the body partially exposed by the wind. Its legs, in their ragged jeans, jut out of the snow. It looks like a teenager, but Paul can't tell. The torso and head are buried. Trembling, he begins to dig, shovelling the snow with leather mitts. Some runs down his wrists, burning his flesh. He strikes the head and stops. Charlie is breathing heavy and wagging his tail. Paul takes a deep breath, inhaling and exhaling the cold, night air. He scrapes along the ears, then down the jaws to the mouth, slowly revealing the frozen, elderly face of Harry Cochrane.

When he's sure it's Harry and that he's dead, Paul scoops snow back over his face and stands for a moment. Harry was a respected man on the reserve. He served in World War Two and was once a band councilor. His wife had died five years earlier. Since then, Harry had lived alone and taken up heavy drinking. He had three children, all grown and scattered. The oldest, Walter, still lives on the reserve. The youngest, Billy, lives in Vancouver. His only daughter, Brenda, works at Indian Affairs. She'll have to come from Regina for the funeral. Paul turns and begins the trek home.

And so the story of Harry Cochrane's death would spread. 'He was drunk,' it would go, 'tried a short cut to his son's place, but passed out and froze. Charlie went for help and led Pete Dieter's boy to him. Good dog that Charlie, but ugly.'

* * *

On another part of the reserve, in a cozy, two story home, Walter Cochrane fidgets with the controls of a satellite dish he installed on the roof. His three sons sprawl on the couch waiting impatiently for him to tune into the TSN broadcast of the Kings-Maple Leafs game. Alan, the older, is a diehard Leafs fan. James likes Wayne Gretzky. After five minutes, Walter gets TSN and the boys rivet their attention to the screen. Walt goes into the kitchen and joins his wife, Shiela, in clearing the supper dishes.

"So you think Phillip's a weak Chief?" Shiela asks, continuing their dinner conversation.

"Not weak. Too low key. It all comes down to the best pitch. Against other chiefs, he can't cut it and they end up with all the funding."

"But he's honest."

"Yeah, that's part of the problem. It's hard finding someone who can throw bullshit at the Feds and not line his pockets at the same time."

Shiela reflects as she stacks the dishes in the sink. "You would be able to get us a new school bus."

"Maybe," he says, "but I couldn't handle working with some of the people that are on the council right now."

"True," Shiela agrees. "You have enough trouble with those two." She nods towards the living room where the voices of Alan and James are rising and falling with the game's action. When Walt looks back at her, Shiela asks, "Is your father coming over tonight?"

"I don't know. He was drunk when he phoned. He wanted a ride over but I told him I was busy. I hate having him here when he's drunk."

"He's still not over your mother's death, is he?"

"Maybe five years isn't enough time."

"Thirty-five years of marriage," Shiela muses. "He might never get over her." Walt grunts as he wipes a plate and Shiela adds, "You've done all you can for him Walt. He has to deal with it himself."

Maybe if I had more help, Walt thinks. Brenda does

what she can, but Billy hasn't phoned or written their dad since their mom's funeral. It's not right, Walt thinks. He hasn't heard from Billy in two years. They never got along anyway, but he could at least say hi to their dad once in awhile. Brenda is the only one he ever talks to.

The phone rings and Walt grabs it, holding one finger in his free ear to hear what's being said. His lips purse as he listens, then he exhales a deep breath.

"How?" he asks, and then, "okay, I'll be right over." He turns from the phone and says simply to Shiela, "It's dad. He froze to death."

"Oh, Walt," she says. She wipes her hands quickly on the dish towel and wraps her arms around him. On the wall the electronic clock with the copper plating ticks the seconds away, the television buzzes in the living room. Walt says in monotone, "I have to identify the body. Then phone Brenda."

Shiela speaks into his chest. "Do it at the station," she says. "So the boys don't hear. I'll tell them while you're gone."

"Right," Walt says. "I'll call you from the station when I know for sure."

* * *

Brenda Cochrane sits in her suburban, Regina apartment idly twirling her long, black hair around her finger and watching a popular, American comedy. She is alone, and has been since her divorce. She had married young, but the dreams that she and her husband had faded as her professional career advanced beyond his, leaving him bitter, and her overworked. As she grew successful, he turned irresponsible. It was a clean break, no children involved. She still dreams of having a family, but now, almost thirty, her work as special project manager at the department of Indian and Northern Affairs commands most of her energy. She dates occasionally, but is wary of relationships. She is still, 'Not ready,' as she tells her friends.

In the beginning, her job at Indian Affairs had created tension between her and Walt, but it was resolved before any real damage occurred. Walt had already lost Billy and he didn't want to lose Brenda as well. And she knew it. She and Billy get along well, mainly because she still treats him as a baby brother; easy to forgive.

Still, the family is disintegrating, she thinks. Billy and Walt don't get along, Billy and her father never have. There was something about Billy's laid back attitude that always bothered them. She remains his only link, calling her when he's depressed, or lonely, his voice at the other end a low, monotone. She calls him too, every two or three weeks. He's doing well in Vancouver. He has a high paying job managing a retail outlet for audio and video equipment, part of a national chain called Video Shed. She's proud of him, and knows her mother would be too. Quite a change from his teenage years.

On the television a commercial for the new Honda Prelude grabs her attention. The first time it grabbed her attention three months ago, she bought the car. She huffs mildly, reminding herself once again to take it to the garage. It's already January and it still hasn't had its winter tune-up. She looks out the window into the cold, night air. The street lights illuminate the blowing snow. Already, the street is white, except where the sewers have melted the snow and left dark circles. Windows on parked cars are snow covered. A hooded man bundled in a parka scrapes diligently at his windshield.

It was a night like this, she remembers, when her mother died. After five years, she can still vividly recall the phone call from her father: his voice restrained and cracked. It was the first time she had ever known him to cry. She was close to her mother, always had been, but she was never as close to her father; perhaps more influenced by him, but not as close. She makes a point of phoning once a month and seeing him on holidays. More for duty than affection. She worries about him though, especially the drinking, which has increased dramatically the past few years.

She lights a cigarette and scans channels with the remote, settling on an American detective show rumored to be getting the axe at NBC. The lead is a muscular, good looking type. She decides to drool for a while, giggling at herself.

* * *

Walt stares at the corpse. It's him all right, no doubt about it, the drunken scowl fixed on his face first by frost, now by rigor mortis. It's a morbid expression, one

18

that will haunt him. He hopes the mortician can fix it, one of the many details and tasks Walt now faces. Frank Ryerson, a mountie, covers the body and rolls it into the wall. He knew who it was, Walt's identification was a mere formality.

"We'll send the body to Regina in the morning," Ryerson says. "For an autopsy."

"He was drunk and froze to death, right?"

"Yup."

"So why an autopsy?"

"It's required."

Walt nods. "Can I borrow your phone?"

"Go ahead...and Walter." Walt turns to him. Frank says softly, looking into his hands, "I knew your old man. He had it rough the last few years, but he was a good shit."

* * *

Brenda is gazing at the muscular TV detective who's chasing a drug supplier down a Florida beach when the phone rings. She butts her cigarette and answers.

"Brenda?" She holds her breath, thinking Walt never phones unless she owes him money or something bad has happened.

"Walt," she says, "how are you? How's Shiela and the boys?"

There's a long pause on the line before Walt answers.

"Fine, under the circumstances." And then before

she has time to say anything he blurts out, "It's dad. He froze to death." Brenda glances from the phone to the TV. In one ear she hears distant static, in the other, gunfire as the TV detective closes in on the drug smuggler. After several seconds, Walt continues, "He passed out in the snow." Brenda doesn't want to hear that. A picture of her father as an unhappy, drunken old man tormented by the memories of his dead wife passes through her mind. She sees him alone in the kitchen, staring out the window and drinking whiskey. Alone in the house she left to pursue a job in Regina, a Honda Prelude, Export cigarettes, and cable television.

"Brenda?"

"What?" she answers, an angry edge to her voice.

"Are you all right?"

"I think so," she says. "Just...you know."

"I'll be in Regina tomorrow. We can talk then. Also, we have to start making the funeral arrangements." Walt pauses and Brenda hears the smuggler scream in pain. "And I guess you should phone Billy."

"Yeah."

"I'm sorry for dumping this on you and I know this isn't a good time to talk. I'll see you tomorrow."

"Walt?" Brenda clears her throat, reflecting on the pain they all suffered five years earlier; of how it brought them together, and nearly tore them apart. "Both our parents are dead now." When Walt hangs up, Brenda looks out the window. It was a night like this, she thinks, a night of heartache and anger; of betrayal and loneliness.

* * *

Billy Cochrane of Kitsilano, executive manager of Vancouver's largest Video Shed outlet, parks his BMW and directs his tires to the curb. From the passenger side emerges Julie, his current lover, carrying two movies on the Beta, half inch video format. Billy's preference. Vancouver's winter drizzle runs down Billy's collar and spots Julie's new Gucci pumps. They dash to the front porch and he unlocks the door.

Julie is a secretary at an office across from Billy's store. She is blonde, five-six, and studies yoga six days a week. At Billy's place, they make vegamite sandwiches and eat anchovy pizza; though most of the time they spend in his bedroom. He pops the first film, Rhonda Reams Rotterdam, into the player while Julie is undressing. He tosses his shorts in a pile with her bra and sweater and joins her in bed.

The film is forty five minutes long, but by the finish, Billy and Julie are engaged in their own erotica. When they finish, Julie asks, "Should we cook something?"

"Let's order out. Chinese."

While Julie scans the phone book for a nearby restaurant, Billy pops the erotic flick out of the player and replaces it with Spike Lee's "She's Gotta Have It."

"You want breaded shrimp?" she asks, cradling the phone against her shoulder.

"Yeah, and lots of chicken balls."

"And lots of chicken balls," Julie repeats. She

hangs up the phone. "Half an hour to forty-five minutes," she announces as Billy lies down beside her.

"We could pick it up, couldn't we?"

"We could," she says, smiling coyly. "Or we could pick up where we left off."

Julie runs the tips of her fingers down the centre of Billy's chest.

"Delivery will be fine," he says.

*   *   *

Brenda butts another cigarette and picks up the phone. Patterns repeat themselves, she thinks, as she dials Billy's number, recalling the phone call she made five years earlier on a blustery, winter night, a night just as lonely as this. As then, the phone rings six, seven, eight times before he answers, puffing as if he's run to the phone.

"Billy," Brenda says, "it's me."

"Brenda?" Billy says, his voice rising. He places one hand over the mouthpiece and whispers to Julie,

"My sister." She isn't quite convinced, but doesn't press the matter. She gets up and goes to the bathroom as Billy rolls to the edge of the bed.

"You picked a bad time," he says into the mouthpiece. "Can I call you back?"

"Oh Billy," she says, her voice cracking. Billy knows something awful has happened before she even says it. "Dad died."

"Oh shit," he says. "Brenda, take it easy."

"Damn it, Billy, he froze," she says, stifling tears.

Billy sits up running his free hand through his hair as Julie pokes her head back into the room.

"What is it?" she asks, but Billy doesn't hear her. A loud ringing rattles through his head and for a moment, nothing in the universe makes sense. Then it passes. His shoulders slouch and his hand drops to his lap. Silence screams through the phone until Brenda speaks.

"We're still a family Billy, you, Walt, and I," she says. Billy remains silent. "Billy, did you hear me?"

"I heard you," he says.

"So?"

"So what?"

"Are we?"

"Yeah," he says impatiently. "I can't talk right now. I'll phone you later."

Billy hangs up, lies back, and stares at the ceiling. Plaster in uneven clumps spreads stylishly from wall to wall. In a corner above the bed, cracks web from the wall out, resembling a map of the reserve. Billy closes his eyes and sees his dad alive and towering above him, a dull, angry look on his face. Billy's eyes pop open. Julie is standing above him.

"You never told me you had a sister," she says quietly, her soft body covered in a chiffon sliding in beside him. She has combed her hair, washed her face, and put on perfume.

"Brenda," he says. He turns to look at her, not knowing whether to hold her and tell her what's happened, or ask her to leave. "She lives in Regina."

Julia purrs beside him. She runs her fingers up and

down his arm, teasing first the hairs on the back of his arm, then the delicate veins on the underside. "I bet," she says, smiling at him, "you're the youngest."

"Yup."

"Parents?"

"Both dead."

"Mmmm," she purrs, running her hand across his chest. He grabs her by the wrist.

"Let's watch the movie," he says, reaching for the remote.

* * *

Billy's flight to Regina arrives fifteen minutes late, thanks to a strong, easterly wind. Brenda waits patiently at gate two. A pack of passengers storm out and race for the baggage carousel, among them three young mothers with screaming toddlers and a dozen businessmen carrying black briefcases. Then the stragglers slowly emerge, Billy among them. In a large, six foot frame, he stands out in the crowd. The brown eyes beneath short cropped hair are darting about. Brenda walks up to him and they hug.

"It's good to see you again," she whispers, "even under shitty circumstances."

"It's good to see you too." Billy looks around, then asks, "Where's Walt?"

"At the funeral chapel. We're having a service for the people who can't make it to the funeral. Mostly dad's legion buddies. We'll go there first."

"I've made a reservation at a hotel. I'd like to go

there first," Billy says.

"You're staying at my place, the funeral chapel is on the way."

"I don't want to be an inconvenience."

"You won't be, now shut up and grab your bags."

Billy obeys. "You're in a good mood," he comments as they walk to her car.

"Both of you piss me off sometimes. Walt wanted to stay in a hotel too. Neither one of you cares that this is only the second time we've all been together in nearly ten years," Brenda huffs. Swiftly, she marches through the icy parking lot, her lips pursed beneath a frown as she stares straight ahead. "Shit, this is a funeral, not a weekend holiday."

Billy has to trot to keep up with her. "Walt's staying at your place too?" When Brenda nods, Billy sighs aloud and says, "Terrific. We can stay up all night and poke each other's eyes out."

Brenda stops and turns to face her much larger brother. Billy, struggling against the slippery ice, nearly collides into her. "We are going to bury our father this weekend," Brenda begins, "and starting now, you and Walt have a responsibility to get along with each other. I'm not going to tolerate any bickering or antagonism between you."

"All right, all right," Billy says, indignantly.

Brenda lightens up. "All right," she says, smiling. In the car driving towards the city they sit, silently watching the streets pass by. The city is flat, lacking rolls. Elm trees stand on boulevards bordering streets that stretch out and meet the sky. Everything is white and grey; the houses, the trees, the roads, even the people. Billy turns to Brenda.

"You like living here?" he asks.

"It's home," Brenda says, shrugging.

"But do you like it?"

"I don't think about it too much."

"Good thing," Billy says, looking at the grimy snow banks. "You ever thought about moving away?"

"No," Brenda says. She looks up from the steering wheel into Billy's eyes so he won't miss the point. "It's home, and it's close to home."

Billy turns and looks out the window, nodding slightly. He remembers the old place well. Chopping wood for the fire and the stove, then carrying the wood in and seeing his mom bent over the wood stove stirring potatoes and stewing beef. There was always bannock and lard on the table, butter in good times. And there was always drink. His father often indulged and the family had to set their patterns around him. His mom always said the old man learned to drink during the war. Billy never cared where he learned, only that he did. Mom made the place a home, his dad worked to destroy it. That perspective has remained. "Well," he says, "so you aren't seeing anyone right now, eh?"

"Haven't found anyone I like," Brenda says. With a yank of the steering wheel, she whips the car off Dewdney onto Albert Street, knocking Billy against the door. Outside, a dozen people huddle at a bus stop trying to dodge flying salt and slush. "But I wouldn't mind having someone to go to once in a while."

"You don't like being alone?"

"I get lonely," she says. "Don't you?"

"I have friends," Billy says.

He watches a Seven-Eleven pass by wrapped in ugly snow and ice. Is this how the city always looked, he asks himself.

"There's only the three of us now," Brenda says, focusing on the oncoming traffic. Billy notes how little traffic there is. A few cars, the occasional bus, all covered in salty grime.

They are silent for the remainder of the drive.

They reach the funeral home, a sombre looking structure surrounded by evergreen shrubs. On the front door reads, Dyck and Son -- a name gracing numerous bus stop benches. They leave the car, stepping into prairie air.

"Fuck, it's cold," Billy blurts, shivering.

"Don't be a sissy," Brenda says.

They walk inside and a pale usher leads them to the chapel where they join twenty or thirty of their father's old cohorts who have come to pay their last respects to Harry Cochrane. Most are war veterans and legion members. Walt is talking to one on the far side of the room, a man with glasses and white hair who Billy doesn't recognize. At first glance, he doesn't recognize anyone. At the front is the coffin, half open to display Harry's upper body. The lower half is closed, and draped with flowers and wreaths. Billy follows Brenda into the room, and overhears Walt.

"So you'll perform the eulogy?" Walt asks the veteran. "Sure, I can say a few words about Harry. Kind ones too." He looks off into the distance. After sixty five years and two wars, he's buried many of his buddies. He attends about four funerals a year, and though he is past the sullen awkwardness that grips people at funerals, he is quietly respectful of the family's feelings. He turns back to Walt, "I could tell a war story or two." Of their unit, Vince is the last surviving member. He has told many war stories at many funerals.

When the minister enters, carrying a cross, a braid of sweetgrass, and a pouch of tobacco, everyone falls silent.

Walt walks over and stands beside Brenda. Billy, on her other side, leans forward to catch a glimpse of his brother and Walt nods in acknowledgement. Billy nods too, then leans back. "What religion are we?" he asks Brenda in a whisper.

"Anglican," Brenda replies. She grabs a hand from each of them as the minister starts into a prayer. Heads bow in unison, except Billy's.

He stares at his father lying in the coffin a few feet away. It is the first time he has seen him in years. They must have fixed him up pretty good, Billy thinks, he looks better than he did at mom's funeral. He thinks back to that event, remembering that his father drank through the entire weekend. They spoke together once. With whiskey breath, Harry told Billy how much their mother meant, and how important it was to keep up the family tradition. It was the first time Billy felt close to his father in many years. The following week, Brenda told Billy that Harry had a black out -- he couldn't remember the funeral.

When the service ends, Walt and Brenda stand by the door thanking those who came. Billy walks up to the casket for a long look at his father. As people leave and the piped music dies out, the chapel becomes quiet, filling the room with an eerie stillness that threatens to overwhelm him. He looks over his shoulder and sees that Vince has stayed behind too. The old veteran tips his head to Billy and moves slowly to his side. "You look like you could use a drink," he says to Billy.

"I could," Billy replies, "but I'm holding out. That stuff killed him."

"It probably did," Vince agrees. "But it helped us get through the war, even if it damned us after." His hands shake and Billy suddenly remembers what his father told him about war -- about shells exploding all around men no more than twenty who saw their friends dropping beside them, horror and pain frozen on their faces. The noise, the smell, the rot, and the agony. Harry's foot ached every spring because of trench dampness. Billy remembers his father often yelling in his sleep. "See you tomorrow," Vince says, leaving Billy alone in the chapel with thoughts about a place where those young men first learned to deal with pain.

* * *

At her apartment two hours later Brenda is busy making tea when Walt saunters into the kitchen and sits at the table. He's wearing a hockey jacket now and looks cold and tired. She places a cup of tea in front of him and he holds both hands around it, as if warming himself. The pattering of water can be heard from down the hall as Billy takes a shower.

"Everything is set," Walt says, "ready for another funeral?"

"Not really," she answers, "but it's serving a good purpose."

"What the hell is that supposed to mean?"

"It's the first time we've been together in five years."

"Like a family you mean?"

"Doesn't tragedy always bring families together?"

Walt shrugs, "For a weekend I guess."

Brenda lights a cigarette and sips her tea. She hears Billy singing in the shower and wonders if he and Walt have had a chance to talk yet. When they were living at home, Walt was Billy's idol. Billy used to ask him about everything and Walt was always patient with his much younger brother. How times have changed. She asks Walt, "Do you mind sleeping on the couch?"

Walt stirs in his seat. "I guess not." He sips from his mug and swirls the tea around in his mouth before asking, "And Billy?"

"Don't start, okay?"

"Okay, but don't expect too much from him and me."

"Could you at least try?"

"It's a two way street."

"You two are so alike, it drives me nuts. He's afraid to tell you how much he wants your approval and you're afraid to give it to him."

"You see a lot of things that don't exist," Walt says.

"Such as?"

"Family unity," Billy says. He's standing in the kitchen doorway and Walt and Brenda wheel at once in his direction. Billy is drying his hair with a large towel.

"Want some tea?" Brenda offers.

"No thanks, is there any coffee?"

"You'll have to make some," Brenda says. She purses her lips toward the doors over the sink and blows a cloud of cigarette smoke in that direction. "It's in the middle cup board."

"There's a full pot of tea here," Walt says, "already made."

Billy looks from Brenda to Walt and then back to Brenda again. He shrugs and puts the towel on the back of the chair. "It's okay," he says, "I'll make some coffee."

Walt snorts as Billy digs in the cupboard. Brenda watches them closely.

"You have decaffeinated?"

Walt sighs audibly but he and Brenda sit in silence while Billy opens the coffee tin and measures out three tablespoons. He dumps them into the filter and pours water into the tank. When the coffee begins to drip Billy sits down and wipes his hair a few more times. The smoke from Brenda's cigarette curls above the table. She searches through it looking for a neutral conversation topic. "So when is Vince coming over tomorrow?"

"Sometime around noon," Walt answers.

"And we're taking your truck?"

Walt's voice is blunt and he taps his fingers on the

table before saying, "Yup."

"Who's we?" Billy asks.

"Vince and me," she answers.

"And us?" Billy asks, nodding his head quietly at Walt, then turning his eyes to Brenda. "How are we getting there?"

"In the hearse," answers Walt.

"The hearse?"

"Yes," says Brenda, "I thought you two should drive out to the reserve with dad. It only makes sense that the two sons should accompany the body back to the reserve. It would also give you two some time to catch up with each other's lives."

"And that's the plan?"

"I'm not complaining," Walt says. "Are you?"

"No," Billy says. He gets up and leans over the coffee machine, checking to see if all the water has filtered through. "As long as there are no screw-ups."

Brenda snorts once, then laughs.

"Remember the time mom and Aunt Josephine decided to clean out the stove and pipes," she says. She turns from Walt to Billy. "And they used that old vacuum?"

Walt leans over the table and shakes his head. "They spread soot all over the kitchen."

"They blew their noses and had black snot smeared on the white toilet paper," Brenda laughs.

"They were scrubbing the walls until midnight," Walt adds.

"That's when we were living in the townsite. I must have been only seven years old then," Billy says.

"And they balled me out for laughing at them."

"How 'bout the time dad got motivated to shovel the driveway. It took him nearly four hours and the next day we got a blizzard and three feet of new snow," Walt says. He lifts the mug to his lips and smiles, remembering. "Shit, was he mad."

"He never shovelled anything after that," Brenda giggles.

"Yeah, he taught me how to do it."

"And after, you had me doing it," adds Billy. "I remember he used to always go hunting with Russ Stonechild. They'd leave around eleven, or as soon as it was dark enough. Him and Russ would sit in the back of that old Chevy pickup and someone would drive for them. Russ would hold the spotlight and dad would do the shooting." Billy pours himself a cup of coffee and sits at the table between Brenda and Walt. "He really knew the back roads, didn't he?"

"Yup. They only got lost once. They were out one night in early September. I guess it must have been foggy or something, but they got lost. And when they woke up in the sunlight, they found themselves fifty yards behind the band office," Walt chuckles.

Brenda laughs too. "And they tried to keep it a secret, but Russ told his brother."

"And half the reserve knew about in an hour," adds Walt.

"Next time they went out, mom gave them a bag of bread crumbs."

Walt and Brenda come close to hysteria with laughter and Billy laughs along too, even though he was too young to remember this event.

"I remember they came back empty handed once and Kookum Mary-Jane gave them hell cause they went visiting," Billy laughs.

"I remember that," Brenda giggles. "They said the only deer they saw that night was Hank Dieter's tractor, so they went to Russ' aunt's place. When they left, she phoned Kookum Mary-Jane and squealed."

Billy sips from his hot coffee as laughter bounces off the kitchen walls. When it subsides, Walt says in a quiet voice, "Once I went with them and the mounties chased us for twenty minutes down the back roads. Dad led them down one after another and they ended up in the slough. The next day, all you could see was the cherry sticking up through the water. They patrolled the hell out of the reserve that summer, but they never did find out who done it."

"He sure knew all the shortcuts, didn't he?" Billy repeats.

"He was always pointing out old roads," Walt says, shifting his weight from one elbow to another and looking directly at Billy, his squinted eyes concentrating on his younger brother's. "Sometimes you couldn't see nothing there but a trail, or nothing at all. He showed me one spot this summer and all I saw was bush. He said the road was older than the bush."

Walt is still looking into his younger brother's eyes when Billy asks, "What happened to him, Walt?"

Brenda leans back and watches her older brother closely. Walt's eyes dip as he stares into the wood pattern on the table. "He must have been walking to my house," he begins slowly, "taking one of his shortcuts through the bush. But it was so damn cold and he was so damn drunk, there was no way he was going to make it. He probably fell and just went to sleep." Walt is tracing a line on the table with his finger.

The phone rings, startling everyone. Brenda gets up to answer it as Billy and Walt lean back and sip from their mugs.

"It was Vince," Brenda says, returning moments later. "He wanted to make sure he had the time right." She sits down amid silence and contemplates another cigarette. Walt's fingers resume tracing, Billy begins tapping his toe.

"I guess it's time for bed," Brenda yawns. The brothers nod their agreement.

"Wanna flip for the bedroom?" Billy asks.

Walt looks up, startled. "Naw," he says, "you take it. I caught some sleep this afternoon."

*　*　*

After he's arranged the covers on the couch and settled himself under the covers, Walt shuts off the lamp letting light from the picture window pour into the room. The rumble from the heating system quits as the thermostat shuts it off. Walt hears the ticking of the kitchen clock now and the refrigerator motor competing with the prairie wind outside. Walt turns to the window. Blowing snow. The wind is bad and he can see the gusts, exaggerated by the street lights. He can hear the sharp whines as well. He can't tell if the snow is actually falling, but he knows the wind will drift what ever snow there is. He hopes the weather won't be so bad in the morning. On the highways in this part of Saskatchewan, blowing snow can hide the road and create ice patches. By the time the heating system resumes its rumbling, Walt is asleep. But it is a light sleep filled with dreams of his father.

* * *

At 8:15, Billy stirs from sleep. His night has been filled with dreams too, but not of his father. When he woke, he was dreaming of a bird. A huge, majestic, black bird that flew high above the forest he was standing in. It could have been an eagle, but Billy isn't sure. All he really remembers is trying to follow the bird through the trees. Sometimes it flew out of sight, then he would spot it again in a small clearing. Finally it led him out of the forest and Billy stood on the reserve. He sits up and shakes his head, running one hand through his coarse, brown hair. Like his father's, it curls at the nape of his neck, but his father's hair was darker, like Walt's.

Billy rises and saunters from his bedroom. Walt, he sees, is still asleep on the couch. The blankets, so neatly arranged the night before, are now dishevelled and scattered. Billy re-heats the previous night's coffee and sits at the table looking into the morning's dawn. The weather is calm now, almost eerily so. The sky, a pastel blue, hangs behind a white snow blanket with curious shadows cast across. Birds whiz by the window from time to time, mostly starlings, landing on barren branches and hydro wires across from the apartment. In a pre-caffeine stupor, Billy thinks about nothing. He gets up, pours himself a cup of coffee, and sits back down. He stretches his lips to the cup and slurps loudly, rousing Walt from another dream.

"You always do that?" he asks. When Billy looks back puzzled, Walt adds, "Slurp your coffee."

"You want some?" Billy pours him a cup. When Walt reaches the table it is sitting in front of him. He sits and gulps at it. Billy asks, "Don't you find it hot?"

"I never notice on the first cup. What time is it?"

"About eight-thirty," Billy says, staring out the window. "Shit it looks cold out there." Their eyes focus on the sky outside, the blue being encroached by thick clouds from the west.

"You should have seen it last night," Walt mumbles.

"Why couldn't we be Navajo or Aztec?"

Walt snorts, "You've been in Vancouver too long."

"You prefer it here?"

"It's a good place to make a living. To raise kids."

"I wouldn't raise my kids here, have them eaten by flies and mosquitoes in summer, crawling through ten feet of snow from Thanksgiving to Easter."

"Since when would you have kids? Vancouver turns people into vegetables. They lie in the rain and stare at the mountains. Their heads are too far into the clouds to think about kids, unless it's by accident."

"And staring at scattered clumps of bush and flat horizons is better? The only thing of any note here is the weather. Enter an elevator and that's all people talk about."

"At least we talk."

"That's all there is to do. What's fun about being cramped up indoors for five solid months every year?"

"What's fun about water pouring on you all year?"

"Why people stay here is beyond me," Billy sighs.

"It's home," says Brenda, standing in the kitchen.

"Not that again," says Walt. He slurps his coffee and looks at the wall, his back to Brenda.

"Well," says Billy, "maybe there's something to it." He smiles at Brenda, "Maybe."

There is a whine outside and they all turn to the window. The sky is still blue in parts, but the wind has returned.

"A funeral in this weather?" Billy asks.

*   *   *

Vince McNabb navigates Walt's truck over the ice-rutted highway that runs north from Regina and eventually past the Berens Landing Reserve. He chats happily about Europe and the wartime escapades he shared with Harry while Brenda listens, strapped tightly to her seat and flinching each time blowing snow obscures the highway. She peers out the truck's foggy windows. The sky has become thick with cloud and snowfall grows heavy as they descend into the Qu'Appelle Valley. Approaching cars have their lights on and some flash them, indicating danger ahead. The snow grows heavier and they are unable to see the bottom of the hill. Brenda grimaces as they approach the white wall below. Noticing this, Vince says, "It's not bad yet." They're on the level where the snow-drifts have piled on the southern slope well above the surface of the highway. "Your father and I drove this way back in '49 through a real blizzard. Drifts as high as the rooftops. By the time we got to Melville, you couldn't see the town. But we made it. Took a bottle of whiskey and six hours though. Roads weren't as good back then either."

"You wouldn't call this a blizzard?"

"Not yet, but maybe before we get to your brother's place."

The road in the valley is slick with packed snow. Brenda can feel the truck sliding sideways on the curves and hear the whirr of the tires rising an octave on the icy stretches as the north side of the valley comes into view. "Will we make it?" she asks.

As a response, Vince guns the truck up the hill, his knuckles clenching the wheel tightly. The truck skids but stays on the icy road for the few minutes it takes to reach the top. When the road again becomes flat, Brenda allows herself to breathe, releasing a big rush of wind. "Walt's got himself a good truck here," Vince says, "better than the old dodge your father and I drove. Reminds me of the time we were trying to take Antwerp. Montgomery was pushing us toward the Rhine at a pretty good clip. Casualties were high and we found one of our boys dead in a yankee jeep. Our NCO said someone would have to take the vehicle up to the front line. It was loaded with important supplies.

Can't remember what though. Probably berets. Anyway, your father and I were tired from the march, so we volunteered. We didn't tell him neither one of us could drive. The unit left and we spent the next two hours trying to figure the damn thing out. Then we spent the next few driving the hell out of it. Damn near killed ourselves doing it too. But the fun ended when the thing ran out of gas. We had ourselves hid pretty good in a thicket when a skirmish broke out. Some shells came pretty close, but not as close as three units of Hitler's boys with our's right on their tail. Seems your father and I had slipped through the German front line. Our NCO was some mad, he had us on guard duty for the next three nights."

Vince has himself a good chuckle, then goes into the fear of landing at Normandy as part of the Canadian first. "Of the hundred and fifty-six thousand men to hit the beaches, eighty three thousand were British and Canadian. The way the damn yanks tell it, you'd think they were the only ones there. Where the hell were they when we played guinea pigs at Dieppe?" Vince pauses and gears down for an ice patch. "Your father hated the war," he continues, soberly. "It taught him to fear, to hate, and to drink. No kid should learn what we had to. When we all went home and made babies, your father held off for several years. He didn't want any more kids getting their first taste of the world in a fox hole. Good thing he wasn't at Dieppe. Seventy-five percent of us were killed or taken prisoner. I caught one in the arm, but it wasn't bad enough to get me home. There's a few good memories of the guys we were with, but the rest is pretty much bad. The ironic thing is, most of us volunteered. There were no jobs at home anyway. I remember jumping into a foxhole outside of Aachen..."

* * *

Walt is driving the hearse, and having a lot more trouble with its long, unyielding body than Vince with the truck. The original driver, a university student, sits beside him, thankful to be a passenger. The hearse glides into the Qu'Appelle Valley fishtailing across the road and stirring up gravel when the wheels hit the shoulders. Billy sits on the far right, his fingers locked tightly to the bottom of his seat. "We should have put dad in the back of the truck," curses Walt, trying to get the hearse back into the middle of the highway.

"That would have looked nice," Billy says. "Arriving at the cemetery and unloading the old man from the back of the truck like a load of wood."

"At least he'd be arriving," Walt says.

The weather, though they aren't that far behind the truck, has become noticeably worse. The snowfall has grown heavier, making it hard to distinguish road from ditch. Small drifts have started to appear and many are now in their path as they make their way toward the north side of the valley. As the wheels cut through them, the hearse lurches and Walt struggles to keep it on the road.

"Hang on," warns Walt.

He floors the gas peddle and the hearse accelerates, fishtailing on the highway. He keeps the vehicle straight and hits the hill at seventy miles an hour. Then curls it over the top two minutes later at twenty-five. At the crest, a violent patch of blowing snow hits them and catches Walt off guard. The hearse strikes a two-foot drift, then spins into a one-eighty degree turn. The university student screams and Walt curses as he claws at the wheel. They come to a stop, tense and speechless.

"Jesus," Walt says under his breath, "whose funeral is this anyway?" He turns the hearse around and continues down the highway. The trio stare into the whiteness, all concentrating on keeping the hearse on the road. The drifts pile high against the farm fences, sometimes stretching across the highway obscuring the centre line and the blowing snow obscures all else, but they keep to the road until they turn off to the reserve. The car bumps onto a snow-covered, dirt road and Walt pulls over. They stare out the windows into blowing snow and bluffs of trees in the middle distance.

"There's a road here?" asks Tim, the university student.

"I think." Walt rolls down the window to see out, but snow blows into the hearse.

"Great," says Billy.

"Just be glad we're almost home."

"Your home," Billy corrects, "I don't live here."

Walt chews on his lip, then his jaw becomes firm. "Let's see how well I really know this reserve. Too bad dad can't help us out."

Billy glances into the back of the hearse, but says nothing.

"This is my first time on a reserve," announces

Tim.

Walt motions at Billy, "It's almost his too."

They proceed slowly, Walt navigating by the feel of the road's surface. He turns right with the road, then left, maintaining their position. "There's a turn about two hundred yards ahead," he explains. "But we have to keep speed up where we can, or we might get stuck in the middle of the road." He starts to say something else but the hearse's front end dips suddenly and the vehicle plummets into a ditch, coming to an immediate stop.

* * *

Vince pulls the truck onto the driveway of Walt's home. He and Brenda leap out and race to the side door holding their hands up to keep the wind off their faces. Shiela is at the door, worry etched in the lines on her forehead.

"Where's Walt? Where's Billy?"

"They took the hearse," Brenda says. "They were right behind us when we left the city." She looks back into the storm. "I was hoping," she says to Shiela, "that it would give them a chance to talk."

Shiela gives her a look, one eyebrow raised, indicating what she thinks of the likelihood of that happening and says, "There's bannock on the table, I'll make some tea. You won't believe how the boys have grown, especially Brent. He's become a tower, almost as tall as his father."

Brenda smiles, knowing it's only been a month

since her last visit, but admiring Shiela's pride just the same. She even envies it. She looks around the kitchen. On the wall hang pictures of Walt's boys, all smiling, but looking more cool as they get older. On a shelf sits an old trophy Walt got for scoring the most goals in a Touchwood Hills Hockey Tournament in the early seventies. Beside it are newer ones, belonging to the boys. Shiela follows her eyes. "That one is Alan's," she says, "for golf. Crazy isn't it? Reserve boys playing golf." She fills the kettle and says, "I suppose I should be proud of whatever they do. It's the changes. I know Walt feels the same way. I guess that's one of the reasons he doesn't get along with Billy. If Billy's skin wasn't so light, Walt would call him an apple." She drops her voice and says confidentially. "He didn't like it when Billy left the reserve, not one bit."

"What about when I left?"

"You were different; you followed your husband."

Brenda bites her tongue, then says, "To me, I think Walt treated Billy just like dad did. Billy didn't have a chance of living up to their demands."

"Maybe, but Walt sure tried living up to your father's."

"Men," Brenda says. She looks into the cup Shiela's set before her and blows into the hot tea before sipping. "Is that why Walt resents Billy?" she asks.

"That, and because he hasn't been around to pick up the slack."

"Just like dad," Brenda says. "But Billy didn't feel compelled to live up to anything, or to stick around for that matter."

44

"That's his decision," Vince says, speaking for the first time. "And I admire him for it."

"Our culture is different," says Brenda. "We take care of our old people. That's the children's responsibility."

"But Billy hasn't even come back to see anyone in years," Shiela states. "Walt resents that."

"We're becoming assimilated," Brenda says. "It's inevitable. But it's destroying families."

"Still," Shiela says, "as long as there is a Walt for every Billy, some of our ways will survive." She's pouring water into the teapot and adds, "Even if the families don't."

* * *

The snow is deep. Walt spins the tires in a futile attempt to free the vehicle while Billy and Tim push. The hearse rocks forward and back and slides sideways a foot before it wedges in a rut and doesn't budge. Walt sticks his head out the window. "We're stuck good," he calls back into the wind. So in a rotation of fifteen minute stints, they take turns standing out on the gravel road waiting for passing traffic. They each learn to concentrate on their sense of hearing and to look down low when they hear a sound, for the blowing snow is less dense near the surface of the road. It is in Tim's third tour of duty that he flags down a snowmobile. When he returns to the hearse, he says, "We're luckier than hell this guy came along. He says no one's out at all. He can't take all three of us, so I'm gonna go. He'll come back for you when he drops me off." Walt nods and waves at the snowmobiler when he turns near the hearse to head in the other direction. In seconds, they disappear into white.

Billy and Walt sit in silence. They have shut the motor off so the whining prairie wind is the only sound. Billy looks into the whiteness of the blowing snow. A drift forms near the hearse and Billy watches the snow pile up and add to it, blowing up and down its slopes like wisps of powder dumped into the wind. Finally Billy says, "You recognize the guy on the skidoo?"

"Nope, too much headgear. Didn't recognize the machine either."

"Just how far from the reserve are we now?"

"About two hundred yards from the boundary. Dad's house would have been the first one on the far right." Walt points off to the right where Billy sees a clump of trees behind the white. "Mine is another five miles up."

"He tried to walk that far?"

"He'd done it many times before."

"But?"

"But this time he was drunk."

"Brenda never mentioned that when she called." Billy is silent for a few moments, then adds, "Though I'm not surprised. She has a tendency to wash things out." When Walt doesn't reply, he asks, "Did he go to your place often?"

"A few times a week. He liked watching hockey games with the boys."

"Was he still a Leafs' fan?"

"Yeah," Walt says. "Poor old man suffered in the last few years, but he never turned his back on them."

They sit in silence once again. Walt turns the car on for warmth, shutting it off every ten minutes to keep the carbon monoxide down. The sky is darker and the wind is growing stronger. Billy blows on one hand, then the other. He turns to Walt. "Was dad drunk a lot?"

"Yeah." His tone of voice tells Billy that he wouldn't have to ask certain questions if he'd kept closer contact with the family.

Billy looks to his right where the road had been visible when Tim left on the snowmobile. Now, there is nothing but white. "They've been gone an hour and a half," he says, looking at his watch.

Walt sighs. "I think we're going to be here for a while little brother."

"They'd let us stay out here and freeze to death?"

"They must think we're okay for the night out here in the hearse. In the morning they'll come for us."

"What if we tried to walk?"

"We'd end up like dad, and they wouldn't find us until spring." Walt's voice has gone soft. Then after a moment he says, "But it's not all gloom and doom." He looks about vaguely. "There's probably some sort of survival kit in here." He zips up his jacket and wraps his scarf tightly around his head. "Take a look around. If there is one, it should be easy to find. I'm going to clear the tail pipe."

* * *

Outside, the storm nearly blows Walt away. The wind howls, driving the snow into his face, each tiny shred of ice stinging his cheeks. The sky is dark, but masked by layer upon layer of blowing snow. Squinting, Walt tries to see the road, but the storm has grown so severe he can barely see the back of the hearse. He can't recall ever seeing one this bad, none in his memory even comes close. Laboriously, he walks to the rear of the car, shielding his face from the piercing snow. The drifts against the hearse have built up to nearly three feet. Moving to the rear of the hearse, he thinks about the night Harry died. He keeps his leather mitts on to clear the snow, feeling each particle of ice that touches the skin on his exposed wrist like a needle into cold flesh. The fumes escape into the storm. Walt watches them, knowing the process will have to be repeated throughout the night. As he moves back to the driver's door, he estimates that with the windchill the temperature is somewhere near minus fifty. His eyelids stick shut with each blink as he stands for a moment looking into the whiteness, then hops into the hearse and closes the door.

* * *

Walt feels warmth against his numb face, a welcome sensation. Billy sits fidgeting with a small kerosene stove. A thermal blanket is wrapped around him.

"I found it," says Billy. "In the glove compartment." He passes Walt the remainder of the kit.

48

Walt takes it and pulls out a small gadget with a meter on it.

"This is important," he says.

"What is it?"

"A carbon monoxide monitor."

They sit in silence as Walt figures out how to operate the gadget. Billy broods as a minute quivering takes over his bottom lip, the first sign of panic. When Walt sees it, he says, "Make yourself useful. Go in the back and see if you can find more blankets."

Billy nods and crawls into the back. He looks around quickly and starts to crawl back toward the seats.

"Check the coffin."

"I can't," Billy says. His face has gone pale and his eyes wide.

Walt snorts, "Just lift the lid and look. It's your father, he's not going to bite you."

Billy takes a deep breath. Would he have the same apprehension if the corpse was a stranger? In the silence, he hears the snow drifting through the night. The snow will settle, but the storm must first run its course. He lifts the lid, preparing himself for the worst, and looks quickly at his father's corpse. In this stillness within the storm, Billy senses tranquility and this feeling banishes the fear. He's surprised. Harry was always a frightful figure to Billy. When they were together working outside or sitting around the house, Harry rarely talked to Billy, but kept up a sheet of silence behind a chiseled, stone face. Billy always feared breaking that silence. But the fear has gone along with Harry. Billy searches the coffin for blankets.

"No blankets," he says to Walt shutting the coffin. "But surprisingly, it's comfortable back here. Not toasty, but comfortable."

"Fine, make yourself comfortable, we're spending the night back there."

Walt climbs into the back and finds Billy reclining casually against the side of the casket. "I thought you might not like this idea."

"Ah, there's nothing to be afraid of," Billy says. He shifts, making his hips more comfortable in the cramped space.

Walt smirks. "Looks like you've had a sudden revelation of sorts."

Billy's eyes become more intense as he stares at his older brother. "How is it you always maintain control?" he asks. Walt doesn't respond. He shifts around, too, waiting to see if Billy has more on his mind before he says,

"If you know what you're doing, you're always in control. Fear is stupid."

"Everyone has fears. Some express them and some don't."

"You never told me you had a license to practice psychiatry." Walt shifts uneasily, searching for a comfortable position. But Billy disregards his casual answer.

"Look," he says, "if you don't express your fears, how will you ever face them?" Walt looks at him without blinking his round, dark eyes.

"What if you don't want to?"

In the silence that follows they listen to the wind's

howl gusting at the hearse, driving more and more snow against them. Walt pulls back a curtain and sees that the drifted snow has piled half way up the window.

* * *

Walt guessed the temperature was minus fifty, but at Melville, Environment Canada's instruments recorded temperatures as low as minus seventy-five. Five miles down the road, Brenda, Shiela, and Vince are listening to reports on the local station. It's been two hours since Tim called and explained how he left the brothers stranded in the hearse. In the kitchen, Brenda, Shiela, and Vince are sipping tea and trying not to think of what might happen to Walt and Billy. Walt's three sons hover at the doorway.

Bannock is on the table, but only Vince is eating. Fear of Walt and Billy dying the same way as their father has driven away Brenda's and Shiela's appetites, though Shiela and Vince engage in happy chatter, reminiscing first about Harry before his wife died, and then speculating on why he began shutting people out towards the end of his life. From time to time Alan fiddles with the radio dial on top of the refrigerator searching for weather reports. When he finds one, everyone stops, causing a sudden lull in the happy chatter. Alan takes the initiative and invites his brothers into the living room to watch NBA basketball. In turn, they invite the adults, who decline politely.

"That's odd," comments Shiela once the boys have left. "I thought Brent and James hated basketball."

"They're trying to make their older brother feel better. Sometimes people get real considerate at times like this," says Vince. "They're just as worried as us, but they're teenagers and they're not sure how to show it."

"Do we?" Brenda asks.

Vince grumbles agreement with her point and adds, "It never gets easy."

"I remember times when Walt and Billy were close," Brenda continues. "Walt used to look out for Billy and Billy used to look up to Walt, more than he ever looked up to dad. They were both afraid of dad. I think their fear turned to anger, and now they vent it at each other."

"Families are a lot like a flock of birds. They fly off in different directions, but when the wind blows strong, they huddle up," says Vince. "They're smart boys, they'll huddle up."

After a while, Brent peeks his head into the kitchen. "It's a great ball game," he says. When he nods to indicate the television, the adults stand and drift toward the other room, happy to have something to distract them.

* * *

It is dark inside the hearse. Billy pushes the thermal blanket off his face and feels the cold that has settled over the hearse. He looks across at Walt, who has fallen asleep, then starts crawling forward, cursing his brother under his breath. Outside, the wind is loud and Billy can barely hear the sound of his progress, but a sudden click and creaking from behind he does hear. He turns and looks over his shoulder, then freezes, seeing the coffin wide open and his father sitting up with a grin on his face.

*   *   *

Billy shrieks and jolts upright. "A dream," he mutters, and leans back, his heart still pounding.

Walt is still asleep and the hearse is cold and damp. Billy will have to turn the engine on so they won't freeze, but decides to wait for his pulse to settle before climbing into the front of the hearse. Listening to the howling wind, he wonders what the weather is like in Vancouver. Probably raining. If they make it through this ordeal, he'll have quite a story for Julie, though she won't believe it. He wonders if he should tell her about the dream too. That would freak her out, then she would believe him.

He is leaning on the coffin when the lid slowly rises and Harry Cochrane sits up, a look of impatience and authority on his face. Billy is stunned and his voice fails him. He wants to reach over and shake Walt awake, he wants to shout at Walt, but all he can manage is to lean slightly toward Walt's slumped body.

"You're wasting your time William," says Harry.

Billy's eyes have never left his father's face, but he looks at the old man as if for the first time. "Aren't you dead?" Harry doesn't answer, but he does smile at Billy, a smile that shows he's enjoying the effect he's having on his son. Billy plants himself against the side of the hearse, his fingers inching along the cold metal. "Go away," he says.

Billy's eyes pop open. The coffin is closed and he's lying on his back, wedged against the side of the hearse. Breathing rapidly, he wipes sweat from his face. The hearse isn't as cold this time. In the darkness, he can see the silhouette of his brother lying across from him. Billy leans over and taps him on the shoulder.

"Walt," he says, pushing his body firmly. "You're not going to believe the dreams I just had."

Walt falls over from the push, and when Billy reaches and grabs for him, he gets a handful of coarse hair. It's stringy and grey, and when Billy turns the head toward the light, his father's features become visible. Billy leaps back hitting his head on the roof. He cries out in a quavering voice. The coffin lid flies open, and this time, it is Walt who sits up in it.

"Jesus," he says. "You sound like a cat in heat."

Billy swallows a lump before he finds his voice. "What the hell are you doing in there?"

"It's warmer," Walt says matter-of-factly. "So I pulled him out. I didn't think he'd mind."

"You could have told me."

"I didn't want to wake you up."

"Great," Billy says. "Thanks for nearly giving me a heart attack." He breathes deeply for a few minutes. When his pulse returns to normal, he senses that the hearse really is cold. Walt must sense it too, because he climbs out of the coffin, announcing, "I'm gonna start the engine."

"Are you going to put dad back in the coffin?" Billy's eyes are still fixed on the yawning casket lid. "Nothing against him, but..."

"Don't be melodramatic," Walt says. He crawls to the front of the hearse and turns on the engine for a bit, then crawls back, stopping halfway to flex a leg and get the sleep out of it. "But if it bothers you that much, we could move him outside."

"Wouldn't that be disrespectful?" Billy asks. "Tossing him outside?"

"As a matter of fact, I was just thinking we could use his body to keep the tail pipe clear."

"That's a morbid thought."

Walt shrugs. "We might as well put him to good use. I don't think he'd want us to die out here." He shrugs again and adds, "It's just a body now. Dad is gone." He looks away and busies himself with getting a good grip on Harry's body. Outside, the sound of wind and snow howling over the fields and through the bush makes every movement seem more ghostly and eerie. When they've maneuvered Harry into position outside, they climb back into the hearse and shut the door on the storm. Ice particles are stuck to Walt's eyelashes, his head is a mess of packed snow. "Feel guilty?" he asks.

"You don't?"

"What I feel is damn cold. And tired," Walt says, easing himself back in the coffin. "So I'm going back to sleep."

After Walt disappears from view, Billy crawls back under the thermal blanket, tucking it firmly beneath his rump and legs before sliding it up and over his head.

* * *

Walt stares into the blackness of the coffin lid looking back through the years with his father, wondering why every memory seems tinged with grey. What kind of relationship did he really a have with his father? He remembers a time when Harry took him out hunting. It was one of the first times Walt had gone so he must have been about eleven years old. They had killed two deer that night and were on their way home when Harry began to talk. "I'm teaching you to hunt," Harry said. "When it's time for Billy to learn, you'll teach him."

Walt swallows, trying to understand why he remembers that speech so clearly. He never did take Billy hunting.

* * *

Billy walks through the darkness, a mist hovering motionless in the air. He hears no noise, only the sound of his feet on the ground, which is firm, but spongy, like permafrost in summer. The air smells of a damp cellar. The eeriness creates wonder in Billy, but not fear. A dim light skirts somewhere off near the horizon and there is turbulence in the mist. Billy stops and watches as the silhouette of a man materializes in front of him. His father.

Billy stares at the figure, then asks, "Where are we?"

"Somewhere between time and beyond space. I can't explain it any better than that, you wouldn't understand."

"Can't we give it a name I might understand?"

"Peace, maybe. You have no fear of me this time."

"You scared the piss out of me."

"When you dreamt I came to you?"

"Yes, in a dream."

"And now you're not afraid. That's good Billy, that's progress." When the silhouette advances and then passes him, Billy sees that the face remains hidden. He turns and follows in the mist which keeps the silhouette partially hidden. The voice comes out of it muffled, saying, "I'm sad about the anger and resentment my death has caused."

Billy says, "I don't resent you," thinking his father is talking strangely.

The silhouette nods and Billy follows it, feeling the spongy ground underfoot. "Billy, did you consider me a good father?" the voice asks. "In your heart, can you say so?" When Billy doesn't answer the voice continues, "I thought so. And yet you came to my funeral."

"You're still my father."

"Do you resent the pressure I placed on you?"

"I regret that it drove us apart. But I suppose as it turned out, it was necessary."

"You mean that you are all successful today?" The silhouette turns slightly toward Billy and he can see that it has relaxed its posture, as if a heavy load has been removed. "It pleases me. I move on feeling proud, able to balance the resentment you hold towards me, all of you."

"That's good, then, isn't it?"

"We were never close, Billy. We could never reach out and grasp one another. We were too much alike and so our wills collided. You always won. You are strong, stronger than those around you think."

"That's what Brenda says."

"Brenda. She could reach the sky, and she reaches both of you. I see how it tears her apart, but you and Walt will reach one another." The silhouette moves slowly away. "We would have reached one another Billy, if we needed to. I always loved you. Now I move on to join your mother and you go back, where Walt is reaching for you."

The silhouette nods at Billy once, twice, and then drifts into the mist where it vanishes. Billy strains his eyes, but all he can see is swirling mist where his father was.

"Goodbye father."

"What?" Walt says. Billy sits up. They are still in the back of the hearse.

"Did you say goodbye to someone?"

"Yeah," Billy shakes his head in wonder. "Our father."

"The bastard made me put him back in the coffin." Walt nods his head for Billy to look, and when he does he sees the corpse, newly frost-bitten, in the casket. Billy looks from one to the other.

"He talked to you too?"

"Couldn't leave me in peace. Had to nag me one

more time."

"Resentment."

"Damn rights. The guy wants us to die like he did. To freeze in the snow. Thought I'd oblige him, so I got drunk too."

"How'd you manage that?"

Walt produces a whiskey bottle, the amber liquid reflecting in the dim light of the dark hearse. Billy whistles. "Where'd that come from?"

"That's the funny thing," Walt says. "It was nestled in the casket. A gift from the old man, I guess you could call it." He passes the bottle across to Billy. "At least," he adds, "we're not gonna freeze to death."

"We're gonna die warm."

"Right." Walt laughs. "Here, have a shot. Death doesn't have to be a cold place."

"Okay," Billy says. He tips the bottle to his lips . Through the thick glass Walt's face is distorted. He looks old and heavy, like the old man, like the old man he's going to become.

*   *   *

"Walt, where's that gadget you had earlier?" Billy says suddenly aware of the passage of time, "the one that measures carbon monoxide."

"Don't worry about that, I know what level we're at." Walt burps and winks at Billy. "It's all relative of course. .08 percent alcohol and you're legally drunk. That's not much. Mind you I'm way over that right now. So was dad." Walt nods toward the casket. "But compared to a hundred percent, it's not much. Same for monoxide. Compared to a hundred per cent, where the level's at right now, it isn't much."

While Walt is calculating on his fingers, Billy boots open the back door, bringing a look of shock to Walt's face as the cold rushes in with swirls of snow and ice pellets. Billy breathes in the clean, cold air, and exhales, hoping to rid his body of the odorless gas.

Walt looks at him out of heavy eyes. "We're gonna die anyway. Shut the door and we'll go comfortably, not the way he did." He leans forward to pull the door and loses his balance, toppling over the bumper. Grappling at Billy's arm for balance, he drags him down too, and they both tumble out of the hearse and into the snow.

"You bastard," Walt mutters. "We're gonna freeze. Just like the old man." His voice is lost in the storm for a moment and then comes back strong. "Christ, isn't that ironic? Dying like that miserable bastard?" He looks at Billy lying next to him in the snow.

Billy's face twists and he says, "What does it matter to you? We're dead anyway, right? Just keep a smile on your face for the next five minutes and you'll still be grinning when they roll you out of the wall."

"You weren't there when they rolled him out. You were never there. Do you know what it was like for the last ten years? Just like it was for the first twenty, except worse. He pushed, he pushed hard, but always at me and you," he says, turning his glazed eyes to Billy. "You ran off, you left him. You left me to him."

"It's not me, man. It's him. He beat you, and you never pushed back."

"You were afraid he'd smother you, so you ran away."

"And you were afraid to do anything he might not like."

"Fuck you!" Walt lifts his arm as if to swing at Billy, but his hand remains suspended in mid air. He sits up in the snow, licking his lips and looking around like a baby child. His eyes have begun to clear. He lifts himself slowly in the drifted snow and climbs back into the hearse. He flips open the coffin lid and drags his father's body out into the night. He throws him into the snow, not far from Billy.

"That's where you belong you bastard, the same place you always left me."

"Walt," Billy says. "Get a grip on yourself."

But Walt is talking to the corpse now, flush with anger. "You had to walk that night, didn't you? You had to try. Just because I wouldn't drive you, you had to try and walk." Walt coughs and looks contemptuously at the corpse, fallen face forward in the snow. "Now you think I killed you. It's never gonna end, is it you bastard." Walt spits accurately at the corpse, his whiskey-tainted saliva dribbling an inch down the pant leg before it turns into amber ice. He drops to his knees. "You bastard," he yells, striking his father in the back. "You fucking bastard." He flips the corpse over and raises his arm to swing at his father's face, then stops. He turns away and looks into the sky. Tears begin streaming down his cheeks and finally, he weeps openly.

He leans back against the hearse and holds both hands over his face. "I'm sorry, oh God I'm sorry. I didn't mean it, I didn't mean it."

"Walt, come on. Let's get inside," Billy says in a subdued voice. He takes Walt's elbow gingerly.

Walt turns and looks into Billy's eyes. The same grey eyes they inherited from their father, eyes that tell what the heart feels. "Don't hate me," Walt says.

"You're my brother," Billy says. "Just like he was my father...our father."

"Right," Walt says. "My brother."

*   *   *

It is dawn. Brenda sits alone on the couch staring at the weather channel on the television screen. In Dallas it is 27 degrees, in Athens, 31. The stereo is on, but the volume is low. She draws on her cigarette and blows the smoke into the centre of the room, watching it curl and spread. She takes another draw and repeats the act. Then she catches sight of a form in the doorway. She turns and sees Brent, Walt's youngest, standing with his hands in the back pockets of his jeans, a sheepish grin on his face.

"Come on in," Brenda says, patting the couch beside her. "What's up?"

Brent takes the place beside her. "Alan and James are arguing." He lifts his eyebrows. "Is that always what happens between brothers?"

"I don't know. I can tell you that people argue." She puffs on her cigarette. "That's a fact of life that you have to get used to." She looks into the boy's serious eyes, eyes as grey as her father's, as grey as Walt's. "But you have to love them both, Brent. Stay out of their differences, but love them. When they need each other, they'll get along fine."

"Yeah," he says, then suddenly changes subjects. "You think dad and uncle Billy will die?"

"Either that," Brenda says, "or they'll find each other."

"You think?" The boy stretches his legs out and lets his head fall back on the couch pillows, closing his eyes. Brenda hears his breathing slow and take on the slow rhythms of the night. His eyes flicker and his fingers twitch, and then he's asleep. Dreaming, Brenda thinks, dreaming out his hopes and fears like we all do. She remembers long silences over dinner in their childhood home after Walt called Billy a patsy and Billy called Walt a jerk. She remembers too how her mother wept and sometimes threw up her arms and went to her bedroom as Walt and Billy began fighting over dinner, and how her father watched with distant interest and nodded approval when one of the boys threw a punch. She felt sick to her stomach. She tried to bring peace but everyone laughed at her, forcing her to bite her lip and retreat into silence until the next time she built enough courage to speak out. One time outside, Walt and Billy were fighting. When Brenda tried to stop them, she caught an elbow in the face and fell to the ground, her nose bloody. She sat and watched them try to destroy each other while her own blood spilled out.

She butts her cigarette and looks down at her

nephew, wondering if he'll be able to cope better than she did. He has the same set to his mouth as Billy, which probably means he'll learn to insulate himself from the pain. Outside, there's a sudden thumping on the wooden steps and Brenda turns to see if Brent has wakened. Then the side door opens and Walt walks in, followed by Billy and a man in a skidoo suit.

"By God, warmth," Billy says, hugging his arms across his chest. There's snow caked to his hair and his cheeks are flushed with cold.

"I told you, eh?" Walt says. He takes his hat off and hangs it on a peg. Then he takes Billy's coat and hangs it beside his own.

"Takes more than a little storm to snuff out a couple of tough guys like us," Billy says. Slowly, he takes his shoes off one at a time, parking his hand on Walt's shoulder for balance as he teeters on the linoleum floor. "I'm a little woozy," he says.

"That's okay," Walt responds. "We'll get you a hot drink and you'll be right as rain in no time. Right Brenda?"

Brenda has crossed the floor and stands looking at her brothers, hands on her hips. "So you survived."

"That's right," Billy says. He squeezes Walt's shoulder as he shifts his weight from one foot to another. "Wouldn't you say, Walt?"

"Yeah," Walt says. He winks at Brenda. "We did." A smile crinkles the corners of his mouth. "And how about you folks?" he asks Brenda. Brenda sidles over between them and grabs each brothers' hand. "Right now, you guys look a lot like dad on my wedding day when he sauntered into the church all covered in snow and red-eyed. He told me I shouldn't marry that bum, then he gave me away two hours later."

"I would have given you away," Walt smiles.

"Likewise," nods Billy.

"I bet you would," Brenda laughs, squeezing both their hands.

RED WAVES

He's been through it before, but it's never easy. If anything, it gets harder, and the odds get higher. He stops to adjust his racing pulse, angry with himself for losing focus. Rule number one: never think about getting caught. He turns to double check his location and suddenly freezes, his hands leaping out against a dark figure. His heart churns as he discovers the mistaken identity, an athletic silhouette of a shadowy mannequin. He dodges through canoes and bicycles on his walk through the sports department.Only one more charge to plant. The words "one more" echo off the walls of his skull and mix with the phrase "getting caught." He reaches the elevators, moving to the middle one of three. He pries apart the doors with a crowbar and climbs into the shaft.

The elevator car is one floor above, a ton of metal hanging over the shaft as he peers up and then down to where the cables are anchored, running through huge, metal pulleys. He grabs a cable and slides down to the floor, then opens his kit and removes a smooth lump of plastic explosives. Gently but firmly, he attaches the explosives to the cables' base, then pushes a bundle of dynamite into the lump. He wipes sweat from his brow, then places a blasting cap in the lump and runs electrical wiring from it to a small timer, which he also embeds in the plastic explosives. He sets the timer and looks above, expecting security or cops to be waiting for him. Getting in and out of the building he finds difficult. His field of expertise is planting the charges. The entrance to the elevator shaft is empty. He wipes sweat off his brow with a tattered, red bandanna. He checks the timer and connections quickly and then climbs from the shaft and races silently and in fear towards the parkade doors of the department store. It is an exhilarating fear where triumph and disaster linger in the dark waiting for a cue. Near the doors, Tracy comes into view, stuffing silver jewelry into a burlap sack.

"What the hell are you doing?" he asks, bearing down upon her.

"Shopping," Tracy says. She looks up at him, her dark eyes filled with defiance and fear. "We've got time. Frankie's not here yet."

"Fuck the petty theft." He grabs her arm steering her to the door. Instead of yielding to his grip, she wrenches away and asks in a harsh whisper,

"What's the big deal?"

"You're forgetting why we're here." He glances over his shoulder and squints at the dark, searching for security guards.

"I know perfectly well why we're here," Tracy continues. "And I don't see how pocketing a few trinkets is going to upset the grand plan."

He cuts his eyes to the red exit sign. "No," he says. "But it may have fucked us up tonight."

He takes her arm again and they leave the store. Outside, it's a freezing, February night. They hear a clicking from a wall on the outside of the store, and then the sound of a dozen alarms from a dozen businesses cracking the frigid air suspended above Winnipeg's downtown core. A cold core.

Near the curb, Tracy stops. "Where the fuck is he?"

They look down Vaughan Street where pedestrians look about in confusion, and then down Graham where a bus driver waits at a stop, looking about with interest. A moment later, a taxi squeals around the corner and Frankie sticks his head out the window.

"Hurry up, get in," he says. He reaches over and opens the passenger's door.

"What the hell are you doing in a cab?" he asks. But Frankie doesn't answer. Instead, he guns the motor and when Tracy bangs the door shut, they squeal into the traffic heading down Portage Avenue.

For a moment there is silence in the cab as Frankie concentrates on driving and Tracy settles on the seat. Then he asks, "Frankie you dumb fuck, what are we doing in a cab?"

Frankie laughs nervously, twisting the steering wheel in jerks as he eyes the traffic ahead.

"All right Frankie, he swiped it for fun," Tracy says. She looks at Frankie and then away quickly because she's still angry about what happened in the store.

"You find that exciting?" he asks.

"Yeah, I find that exciting. I find this whole thing exciting." Tracy looks out the window. End of conversation, though all three of them know that getting picked up on a stolen vehicle charge is two inches away from an arson conviction.

The taxi winds clumsily through the downtown streets. Near Garry Street, Frankie weaves past a parked car and when he turns off Portage, the front wheels strike the curb. The intensity on Frankie's face bleeds through his pores in sweat.

"Relax, Frankie, get us there in one piece."

"He's all right," Tracy says. She shifts her weight into a more comfortable position and then locks her door. "All cabbies drive like this."

When the cab grinds to a halt by a large, downtown hotel, Frankie sighs and wipes sweat off his face with his sleeve. "I'll get rid of this thing," he says. He waits until they're out on the curb and then whips the cab into traffic on Smith Street.

Inside, he closes his eyes and leans against the elevator wall. He's falling from his adrenaline high into the pits of relief. It is a short fall, for the days ahead will be filled with different dread -- the waiting for the doors to burst open, the nervousness of seeing a cop, the fear that at any moment, his freedom could end. Fear will hang over him like an anxiety-drenched cloud sometimes for days, sometimes weeks.

He watches the numbers rising with the progress of the elevator. Beside him, Tracy looks excited, her eyes wide with expectation. The bag with the silver jewelry is still clutched in her hand. She's never nervous about these moments. She looks at him and shakes her head. "Why are you always so uptight about these shows? They should be exhilarating," she says, leaning against the elevator wall.

"Exhilaration is a short-lived feeling."

"When the feeling hits, you should pause and enjoy it. Honestly," she adds, "you're becoming a nervous wreck. You gotta learn to relax." When the elevator reaches the seventeenth floor, they slip out and pace down the carpeted hallway to room 1705. They enter their room and Tracy falls onto the bed. They leave the lights off. He looks at his watch, then out the large picture window facing the west. Below, the streets are dotted with cars flowing into the downtown district. To the north, the sky is filled with pale stars fighting against the city lights. Westward, he can see as far as The Bay where red lights flash from several police cars forming a barricade around the stone structure.

From the bed, Tracy asks, "Is it time?"

"Almost."

"This is my favorite part."

"Uhuh."

When Tracy rises from the bed, they walk out onto the balcony. The frigid north wind howls, almost obscuring the distant sound of the sirens. In silence, they stare across the rooftops at the majestic block of cement built early in the century by the Hudson's Bay Company, its eight floors aglow with orange from the lights below. From their vantage point, its roof is dark except where light catches the metal of its ventilation outlets.

"It was too close tonight," he comments.

"We're still new at this, it'll get better."

He glances at his watch. The charges were set for eleven-thirty, his watch reads eleven twenty-nine. He takes Tracy's hand. "Any second now," he says. Then the distant building erupts, shedding it's mortar skin and sending waves of fiery red into the night sky. The deafening blast bounces off the side of the hotel with a crack.

"Yeah!" Tracy shouts triumphantly. He can feel her excitement in the way her fingers grip tightly around his hand. He watches the cloud of blaze in silence. The fiery red reflects in his eyes, turning them first a dark red and then yellow as the flames light the city. His mouth tightens as his teeth grate against the each other. His fist clenches and unclenches and he removes his bandanna, breathing deep and fast. He turns suddenly to Tracy and seizes her in a rough embrace, kissing her passionately. She responds with a desperate passion that equals his, digging her nails into his flesh. "We really are perverted," she pants as they rip at each other's clothes. Her bra falls over the balcony rail as they move inside and fall to the bed.

* * *

"Are the actors ready?" Wayne asks urgently. He's been thinking that if they delay any longer the crew will run into overtime plus a meal penalty.

There is a pause while Jan, the second AD, consults with the makeup department. "Five more minutes."

"Right. Steve?"

"Yeah?" responds the third AD.

"Tell Julie we're ready," Wayne says, referring to the film's director.

"Where is she?" asks the third AD.

"How should I know, find her," Wayne barks.

"Wayne?" The enquiring voice belongs to the production manager trainee, doubling as location manager.

"What?" growls Wayne.

"We're close to that meal penalty."

Wayne checks his watch. It's five-thirty. According to the ACTRA bible, the meal has to start at six. He grabs the production board and double checks the length of the scene.

"The scene is only one and one eighth of a page, with luck we should get into a conclusion of shot situation," he reasons.

"We can't afford overtime on the actors."

"If they take a break now, the entire crew will be on overtime," Wayne says, then shoves his talkie back into his belt as he looks at the set, a restaurant at a street corner. He notices something is wrong and races over to the camera operator who is setting his frame.

"Do you see that red pickup?" Wayne asks. The camera operator nods and Wayne grabs for his talkie.

"Steve," he shouts.

"Yeah?" comes the voice, not on the talkie, but from behind. Wayne turns and sees his third standing alongside the director, Julie Daniels.

"Hi Julie. The camera's in position, we're just waiting for the actors and we're a bit pressed for time. Steve, have someone move that truck the hell out of there." Steve, the third AD, scampers off and Wayne turns back to Julie. "The extras are in the restaurant if you want a word with them," he says, raising the talkie to his mouth. "Jan? Are the actors ready?" he asks. "They're on their way."

"Great, do they have their ice cubes?"

"Yup."

February is a cold month in Winnipeg, the temperature often dipping below freezing. Actors suck on ice cubes so their breath isn't caught on film.

Wayne sticks his talkie back in his belt and walks over to Gerry the sound recordist. "Almost ready?"

"Yeah," says Gerry. "Russ is getting the boom mike in place now."

"Tell him to watch for shadows this time," Wayne says, warning in his voice. As he speaks he sees the red pickup truck drive off and the actors reach the set. Julie comes out of the restaurant. "Let's run through the blocking once more," she says.

The actors take their positions as Wayne reaches for his talkie again. "Steve, we're almost ready to roll." He shoves the talkie back in his belt and approaches Keith. "Are you happy?"

Keith broods while stroking his beard. "Yeah, we're set."

Wayne's head spins about. Everyone seems ready. "First positions please," he yells, grabbing his talkie. "Lock it up P.A.'s, we're rolling." Cars are stopped as the actors take their spots.

"Roll sound," Wayne shouts.

"Speed," reacts Gerry the sound recordist.

"Camera."

"Mark," blurts the camera operator. The clapper loader jumps in front of the camera with the clapper.

"Scene 71, take one, mark." CLACK!

"Action!" shouts Julie.

Wayne grits his teeth as the forty-five second shot begins. He takes a pill for his ulcer, washes it down with coffee, and lights a cigarette. He still has another fifteen seconds to relax. He takes a few deep breaths.

"Cut!" shouts Julie.

"Well?" asks Wayne. Julie hesitates, her hand stroking her chin.

"We're getting close to a meal penalty. Can you live with it?"

"It works for me," she replies.

"Okay, we're moving in for close ups," Wayne yells. He grabs his talkie. "Let traffic go and release the extras," he bellows for all to hear. Car motors roar and the production machine resumes. Wayne sighs for a moment, then is tapped on the shoulder by Keith.

"We've got problems," says Keith pointing up at the sky where Wayne sees clouds moving in. "We can wait for the sun or I can light it," Keith says.

"There's no time to wait," Wayne spits. Keith turns and shouts to the gaffer.

"Bring in a 1250 HMI."

Wayne feels a sharp pain and puts his hand on his stomach, then shakes his head. "What a way to make a living," he mutters to himself.

* * *

It is late. The day's shooting has come to an end and Wayne is on his way home. "Christ," he says.

"What a day." He looks out the window of Janet Fontaine's car at the bare elm trees flying by.

"That wasn't too bad," Janet says. "We had a small meal penalty, but if we doctor the sheets, the union won't know the difference." Janet is the second assistant director and she's dropping Wayne off at home.

Wayne puts his cheek against the cold window, waiting for three aspirins to kick in. "We were lucky the sun came back, Keith would have lit the entire street," he sighs. "And tomorrow doesn't get any easier."

"You get yourself too worked up," Janet says with sympathy as she watches his head rattle against the window. "You should learn to relax."

"I'm always relaxed, except during film production," Wayne groans, clutching his stomach. "It's an intense time and we've done too many in the past year."

"Well, the shoot's almost over," Janet says. "Pretty soon you'll be a journalist again."

"I'm looking so forward to that," Wayne says tilting his head to look at the sky where clouds hide the moon.

"I wonder what state our magazine is in," Janet muses, steering the car as it slides around a curve in the road.

"Don't you love the Native multimedia business?"

Janet pulls the car into Wayne's driveway. He looks up at his house and sees that all the lights are off.

"See you at six-thirty," she chirps.

"Don't remind me."

"Goodnight."

When Wayne gets out of the car and Janet drives off, he checks his watch. It's ten forty-seven. Theresa must be asleep. She hates it when he works on films, and he can't blame her. During production, the film soaks up all his time and energy, leaving no time for her and the kids. He enters the house and closes the door softly behind him, then walks upstairs to their bedroom. Theresa lies serenely in bed. He kisses her on the cheek and she twitches lightly.

"How was the day?" she asks.

"Productive."

"How many days left?"

"We wrap on Thursday."

"Good," she says, her lips falling sloppily back together. Wayne smiles, loving it when he sees her this way. She looks even more beautiful, her long, black hair piled up on the pillow. "There were some calls. You'd better check your answering machine," she says, her tongue running across her lips as she slurps, pulling them back in. She dips back into sleep and Wayne goes downstairs to the kitchen. He opens the refrigerator and takes out a jar of mayonnaise and a loaf of bread, plus a tomato, a head of lettuce, and a package of sliced turkey breast. He decides to leave his messages until the film is in the can, but broods over a disturbing phone call he got the night before. The phone rang seven times before he answered it. He said a drowsy hello and a voice he didn't recognize came on.

"Mr. Wayne Weenusk?" Wayne mumbled an affirmative and the caller cleared his throat. "You don't know me, but I have some information that might interest you."

"What?" Wayne asked, thinking the caller sounded a lot like Daffy Duck. There were several moments of silence before the caller spat out, "The Hudson's Bay was bombed by a Native terrorist group."

Wayne was suddenly wide awake, unbelieving, but awake. "Who is this?" he asked.

The caller wouldn't say his name, but he spouted off a pile of facts to support his claim. Wayne believed none of it, but jotted it down in shorthand anyway. He could always check it out later. But as the caller continued, Wayne grew less skeptical. There had been a similar bombing in Toronto two months earlier, only it was a brewery, and two months before that, a Catholic church was blown up in Montreal.

"What do the Hudson's Bay, the Catholic church, and alcohol have in common?" the caller asked.

"I need more than that," Wayne said.

"That's all I can give you," the caller answered, then hung up. Wayne finished his shorthand notes, then put them on the fridge and went back to bed. He tried to think the theory through, but was too exhausted.

"Who was it," Theresa asked, barely awake.

"Daffy Duck," said Wayne. He was asleep seconds later.

Wayne puts his sandwich on the kitchen table and digs in the fridge for a can of coke. Then reaches on top of the fridge and grabs the notes he made the night before. He returns to the table and reads them through, having trouble deciphering his scrawl in places. When he finishes, he pushes the little notebook aside and grabs his sandwich. Terrorist bombings in Canada? Not since the FLQ crisis, or the Squamish Five. But this time, a Native group may be responsible. Not openly of course. He's heard nothing about terrorism surrounding The Bay explosion, but what if the caller wasn't just a crank? Could a Native group be striking out against oppression? Among a sea of moderates who brought ''Red Power'' back after twenty-five years of conservatism, have radicals sprung up?

He bites into his sandwich. The tomato's juice drips out the other end onto the table. Wayne can sympathize with whoever might be behind it, if anyone really is, but could he condone their actions? The church, alcohol, and the Hudson's Bay have done irreparable damage to Native people, but what good is blowing up buildings going to do? It would be a hell of a story, though. The most exciting news on the Native front since Wounded Knee.

He walks into the living room with his sandwich and coke. His mind drifts from terrorism to the look on Theresa's face when she awoke, to the brutal schedule of film production, and finally to the Native Communications Network where he works. He collapses on the velour sofa with a grunt and flicks on a lamp.

''Hi Wayne.''

The voice startles Wayne and he nearly chokes on his sandwich. He looks up into the low light of the living room. Across from him is a figure sitting on the love seat. It's his older brother, John.

"Holy shit!" Wayne puts his hand over his heart. "You scared the shit out of me."

"Sorry." John stands, his face thin and weathered. "Theresa was already asleep, so I just walked in."

"Well, it's good to see you." Wayne stands and crosses the floor to hug his brother. On his clothes he smells must and grime. "Where have you been hiding?"

"I was in Toronto for a little while," John says. He releases Wayne and sits down again. "Still roaming mostly."

"How long has it been? A year?"

"About that."

"Shit, it's good to see you again. You want a coke or something?" John lifts his hand, showing Wayne that he's already helped himself. Wayne chews on his sandwich and drinks from his coke, all in preparation for his next question because he knows John is more than just an innocent drifter. "So what brings you into town?"

"Nothing really, just passing through."

"Do you need a place to stay?"

"Just a few days, maybe a week. I'm short on cash, but I could help out in other ways."

"Well, the washer needs fixing." Wayne broods. He rarely sees John anymore, but when he does show up, it's always unannounced. He wishes he was more a part his brother's life, or at least he could know more about it. "And the walks need shovelling. I've been busy on a film lately and haven't had time to look after the place."

"Then it sounds like I came along at a perfect time." John takes a gulp from his coke, gripping the can tightly. He wipes his mouth nervously and sits up making his body rigid.

"Yeah, and Theresa could use the company."

"So what's this film you're working on?"

"Another production from the organization I'm working for. It's a one hour drama about a Native family in transition from the reserve to the city. I helped write the script."

John smiles. "You've come a long way from the kid who used to follow me on protest marches and to Pow Wows."

"That's where my education began," Wayne says. "From Cache Creek to the riot on Parliament Hill." He laughs, reflecting that it's true. He learned more in two years on the Pow Wow and protest trail than he did in sixteen years of school.

"You remember all those times?"

"Yeah, I remember. They were the most frightening and most exciting times of my life. Only one regret though, I wasn't at Wounded Knee."

John drinks his coke. He's wearing a bandanna around his neck and it rises and falls as he swallows. "You were too young and it was too dangerous," he says. "A lot of people got hurt, everywhere."

"Like mom," Wayne says.

"That was a long time ago."

"Think we'll ever know the truth about her?"

"I doubt it," John says, denting his coke as his grip tightens. "The R.C.M.P. have probably destroyed her file."

"That leaves a lot to speculate on."

"Speculation can lead to insanity, we both know that."

Wayne smirks. "You were always a good philosopher, and a good brother. I was only eleven when mom left and you took care of me instead of shipping me away to relatives. Have I ever thanked you for that?"

John laughs, "About a hundred times." He pauses to cover a yawn and Wayne sees a wide cut running from John's middle finger to his wrist. John spits out his yawn and adds, "You would have done the same for me if the roles were reversed."

Wayne yawns with a growl, realizing how exhausted he is. Three more days of production, he thinks, barring any screw ups. God how he hates film. Tomorrow, another headache along with the insanity of production: swallowing the calm and chewing the meek. Yuck! He chuckles to himself, knowing he quibbles this way during every production. When the film is in the can and the final rushes are over, he will be relieved, and feel, too, some loss and exhilaration all at once. Then the production will slip into memory. "I'm tired," he says, getting up. "I'll be busy for a few days, but we can spend some time together on the weekend. You know where the blankets are, eh?"

"Yeah, thanks," John says, watching his brother walk to the stairs. Wayne waves a welcome without looking back.

* * *

John smiles. He can't help but feel proud of Wayne's accomplishments. A flourishing career, a family, nice house -- the Canadian dream, he marvels. He's been critical of Wayne in the past, accusing him of selling out. But such criticism usually rolls off an envious tongue. They stood at the same crossroads years ago. Wayne chose one direction and John another, both knowing the consequences of each other's choice. Wayne went on to get a degree in Journalism, and John, in the spirit of their grandfather who served in World War II, joined the Canadian Armed Forces.

He lies down on the couch, choosing to forego any blankets. He served five years in engineering building bridges, towers, handling explosives, then quit when promotion always went to others, but never to him. After that, he drifted from one menial job to another, becoming involved in Native rights groups whenever he stayed in one place long enough, and in roles that didn't require a law degree. The movement, he observed, had become too bogged down with bureaucracy, a fact that caused him endless frustration. And through it all, the acrid memory of his mother never subsided. Despite his advice to Wayne to let old memories die, it still hangs above him like a maddening stench. He shakes his head to clear his mind. An insomniac, John gets up and walks to the kitchen. He turns on the tap and pours himself a large glass of water. Something to sip on while he lies awake, staring into the darkness and trying to rid his mind of the images of his mother. He opens the fridge and looks into the freezer for ice, then turns and heads for the door, but stops as something on the kitchen table catches his eye. He reaches down and grabs Wayne's note pad. The shorthand scrawl is illegible, but written across the bottom in question form is, "Native terrorists responsible for bombings in Winnipeg, Toronto, and Montreal?" John puts the pad back on the table and stares out the kitchen window, his left eye twitching slightly.

* * *

The arrival of the weekend finally allows time for Wayne and John to spend some time together. Saturday afternoon, John is in the basement finishing the work on the washing machine. When Wayne comes down the stairs with two beers, John tightens the last screw, securing the panel over the motor. "That should do it. No more dirty laundry."

"Right," Wayne says, handing John a beer. "Now if we could only get rid of all our dirty laundry."

John laughs. "Your personal supply or do you mean it in a broader sense?"

Wayne leans against the dryer as John takes a swig of beer. "I was thinking of our national leadership," Wayne says, looking into his brew for answers. "Do you think the Federation of Indian Nations can survive if Indian Affairs is dissolved?"

"Sure, but we need leaders who are educated and know the system," John says. "Not bums shouting empty promises."

"Is that the problem?" Wayne asks. "I thought we tried to move too fast."

John raises an eyebrow at his younger brother. "I always thought we moved too slow."

They talk about the American Indian Movement. John laments its demise, but Wayne recognizes it was essential to move away from the protests and into the government's own game to secure better rights for Native people. Indian Brotherhoods became assemblies and confederacies.

"That's when we lost our soul," John states. "We modelled ourselves after a foreign system."

"We had to in order to survive," Wayne answers. He sympathizes with his brother's frustration. Native political organizations became too bogged down with bureaucracy, sometimes floundering under their own weight as leaders lined their pockets. But those organizations were essential as self-government was implemented. "Unity came slow because the government treated us as one lump of people. The Cree, Ojibway, Mohawk; all had to get along and play the game to be taken seriously."

John groans into his beer. "If band chiefs and councils knew anything about responsibility, everything would have been a lot easier and we'd have more to show for it."

"We have economic networking of reserves."

"We barely have national unity. The government put everything back in our hands hoping we'd screw it all up. Judging by the people we have in power now, they won't have long to wait."

Wayne shifts his weight on the dryer. "There are always problems to iron out with big change," he says. "I just wish we had a free Native press."

"We've learned all the bad things from the white man's government: deception, misinformation, patronage."

"We'll get it together," Wayne says with confidence.

"We need a kick in the ass," John concludes.

They spend hours talking about old times and the future for Native people. Then the weekend ends. John trucks off with his army issue duffle bag, Wayne drives to work with his briefcase.

*   *   *

Wayne sits in his office sipping juice and looking over newspaper clippings of The Hudson's Bay bombing. He'd prefer coffee to juice but his body needs the nourishment after the caffeine and alcohol of the weekend. His feet rest on his desk under a large window overlooking market square, one of the few offices of the Native Communications Network that has a window. On his desk sit pictures of Theresa and his two children, Jason, seven, and Jessica, four. He'd wanted one more child but Theresa set the limit at two. End of conversation.

The office is sparsely decorated, save for a few posters, some plants nearing death, an overstuffed waste paper basket, desk top computer, and a mound of dishevelled papers on a solid oak desk. When Janet

Fontaine walks into his office and dumps two more files on his desk, Wayne asks, "What are these?"

"The clippings and police statements from those two bombings you asked for. Try not to lose them." She nods at his cluttered desk.

"Right," Wayne answers, already looking through the files. Janet clears a spot on his desk, then sits down. It takes Wayne a moment to notice she's stayed. He looks up at her over the edge of a "Toronto Star" cut-out. "What?" he asks.

Janet regards him curiously. "What are you digging into?"

"A long shot," he says, wondering if he should fill her in. She waits expectantly. "I got a phone tip," he begins. "It might be a crank, but I thought I'd check into it to be safe."

"And?"

He leans back with resignation. "So far, it checks out."

"It's the Hudson's Bay explosion," Janet says. Wayne nods and Janet continues, "It was a bombing and whoever's responsible did these other two." She points at the clippings on his desk. Wayne is mute, but his eyes shine affirmation. "Who's responsible?" Janet asks.

"The Bay, alcohol, and the church. Think about it," he tells her. Janet turns and stares out the window. She lets out a breath and raises a brow.

"This could be big," she marvels. Wayne nods as she stands up and paces across his office. "What do you think?"

Shrugging, Wayne says, "It could still be a crank,

but so far, everything's checked out. It sounds feasible."

"Worth more investigation?" she asks, staring into a Meeches print beside Wayne's degree.

"Yeah," Wayne admits. "Although I'm hesitant. What if it's true and what if we break it?"

Janet eyes the sweeping, blue lines of the painting. "Take as much time as you need, but keep a lid on it. Does anyone else know?"

"Just the caller."

"Good. There's a meeting in half an hour. See you in the board room." Janet turns from the print and walks out of the office, shutting the door behind her. Wayne leans forward and begins reading the newspaper clippings.

* * *

Wayne sits in the board room staring out over Albert Street as he waits for others to file in. Across the square, he watches snow wisp over roof tops driven by Winnipeg's famous wind. Funnelled by four towers at Portage and Main, the wind is stronger now than in the era it gained its notoriety. The notorious wind. Wayne wonders where John is. He'll get a call from Rapid City or Vancouver one of these nights, if he's lucky. A sheet of snow blows past the window as Wayne turns his focus back to the board room. He wonders why they need this meeting. The staff for the newspaper and the magazine isn't large, but protocol requires the formality of meetings, events that Wayne looks upon with the same regard as coffee break mutter or lunch time chatter. Nothing of significance ever comes out of them, nothing worth remembering. It is no doubt a different experience for Janet. A chance to check up on what others are doing and to wield her power. He smiles as she crosses the room to join him. He always puts her through hell on the film shoots and though she always threatens to get even, she never does. When everyone's in the board room; Janet, Walter Cook, Andrea Harper, the magazine's assistant editor, Jack Spence, the journalist, Judy Watts, trainee, and Jeff Starr, the photographer/cartoonist, they sit and look at Janet.

"This shouldn't take long," she says, "which is good because we have a lot of work to do. According to Walter, only half the magazine has been laid out, but all the submissions are in. In case you're wondering," she comments with a scowl, "the feature this month, as chosen by the interim editor, is the transportation network." She clears her throat and turns to Walter.

"Seems there's been a service reduction in Northern Ontario," Walter explains. A big man, he clasps his hands together on the table as he talks. "So we've written about how the transportation network has grown in the last few years to serve the reserves' trade and how reduced service affects it. We're stirring the pot." Walter smiles when he says this and he turns to Jack to make sure his point is clear. Jack smiles weakly. "If the article works then we'll bring pressure on Ontario from other provinces to get their act together."

"Sounds like the long way around," Janet blurts. "Why not do a story on the breakdown itself, then explain that the bands up there are pissed off because the Federation still hasn't come through with the money for a new community college, even though four more have been funded on richer reserves in Southern Ontario and Alberta."

While the two managers develop a power struggle, Wayne considers the pros and cons of either side. The Northern Ontario bands feel cheated, so they're not strongly motivated to serve the networks everyone else has worked so hard to establish. He hopes Walter has enough brains to see the story Jan's way.

Walter scratches his chin in contemplation. "That's right," he comments. "But your article, Janet, would only add to the rift that already exists. And the last thing we want to do is put the unity of the Federation at risk, not to mention that our board of directors would never allow such a story."

Janet smiles curtly, but her eyes don't. "I have a strong, working relationship with our board. As editor, they trust my skills and experience. The stories we produce are as relevant and honest as possible for a Native publication."

"I think our priorities should lie with the well-being of our networks," Walter says, scratching.

Janet, still smiling, says, "Truth is the truest way. If the reserves know the real story, I trust the right thing will be done. Let's not play big brother here."

"We have a responsibility."

Janet traces the end of her pen across the lines on the note pad in front of her. "Perhaps we should discuss this more at the close of this meeting so we can get on to other business." Walter looks glum as Janet begins on another topic. She catches Wayne's eye and winks as she starts. "Wayne, I think I told you a couple of days ago that Jack has been looking into the Hudson's Bay explosion. Now that we know it's a bombing I want you to take over that assignment. Jack, you'll help me research for my interview with the new Minister of Indian and Northern Affairs. Get me lots of background and history. This guy's a racist and I want plenty of ammunition in case it gets dirty, which I hope it does."

"What angle is the interview going to take?" asks Jack, a plump forty-year-old with thick glasses.

"I'll be asking him what it's like to be appointed minister of a department that has shrunk by ninety percent over the last ten years, and what the government's assessment of the Federation's performance is so far."

"I think we have a problem here," says Walter, his fingers still raking at his chin. "Jack hasn't looked into the explosion."

Janet turns and glares at Walter. "Why the hell not?"

"I was acting editor at the time and I didn't see how the bombing had anything to do with Native people. Maybe you could tell me."

While she hesitates, Wayne casts Janet a concerned glance and she cuts her eyes once to his, indicating by a quick blinking action that she won't let him down on this one.

"Since the Hudson's Bay Company has played a major role in Native history, I thought the bombing of one of their stores might be worth mentioning. An evil receiving its due, so to speak."

Walter gouges at his chin. "This magazine is supposed to be a forum for issues concerning Native people, not a lynch rag. We will not glorify violence and vengeance."

"We're not going to glorify anything," Janet seethes. "The Bay was bombed. That is news."

"Embarrassing Canada's oldest department store, regardless of their past, is not going to accomplish anything positive. It will entrench their hatred towards Native people even more."

"Look, my own feelings on this is to find who bombed them and shake that person's hand. Obviously, that wouldn't be a wise thing to do. But the act was done. By reporting it, we're merely informing. If the Bay sees that as an act of vengeance and decide they will no longer issue credit to Native customers, then fuck 'em, but I'm sure they won't. If I were vengeful, I'd print an article blasting the monopoly they had on our reserves." Janet pauses and lights a smoke, then turns to Wayne. "The story runs."

The room is still and expectant. Eyes dart from Janet to Walter. Dropping his hand from his chin, Walter leans back and lets out a little sigh. Janet blows a wisp of smoke across the room. Wayne likens it to the snow blowing outside. "What about efforts to turn control of northern stores over to the bands," Walter says. "We should do a story on that." Janet nods. The room relaxes.

"Jeff," Janet begins. "We'll need pictures for the

transportation feature, shots of trucks with the Federation's logo, that type of thing. Andrea, you and Judy work on the layout and get it finished. That may mean overtime. Walter, you and I have some things to discuss, we can do it in my office. If there are no questions, this meeting is toast."

Janet rises and strides purposely from the table.

*　*　*

At lunch break, Wayne asks Janet, "What did Walt baby have to say?" They leave the brick building that houses the Native Communications Network and walk towards Market Square, joining a throng of pedestrians in a midday march for nourishment.

"He reminded me of our responsibilities."

"You mean keeping our asses covered."

"I mean keeping our grant money."

"Did he ask about the bombing story?"

"No, but I suppose there was a warning about it some where in his speech. I wasn't listening too closely."

"And you won't be telling him what I'm really up to?"

"No way. He'd spike it in a minute," Janet says, her eyebrows dipping into a frown. "Do you know where to start with it?"

"I'll cover the police and R.C.M.P. statements first. If there's any evidence to support our theory, I'll start tapping the political grapevine. I have a lot of radical friends. If a native group is involved, someone should have heard something."

"It's a long shot, isn't it?"

"It's a mystery. First we get an anonymous tip, like it's a big episode, and then nothing. Silence."

"It's strange," Janet says. "And frustrating too. What we need are facts, a statement at least."

"Maybe they don't want publicity." Wayne points to a stairway and they enter a basement deli.

"Then what do they want?"

"What do they want?" Wayne repeats. He looks around the room and finds a menu posted on the wall. Beside it is a chalk board advertising the day's special. Halibut steak. As they wait to be seated, he studies the patrons. And as they study him back, Wayne notices he and Janet are the only Native people in sight. Some things never change.

* * *

South of Portage Avenue, John Weenusk, wearing a rumpled, green parka, leaves a red brick building. He pauses to study a set of keys in his hand, then shoves them into a pocket. Squinting from the sun's glare, he begins a march over snow-encrusted sidewalks that carries him across Winnipeg's downtown district. Half an hour later he's standing near the shattered ruins of The Bay. He studies the burnt building for a while; the charred wooden structure, shattered glass, melted iron, police and fire fighters poking through the debris. Then John stares across the street at a new luxury hotel. Years ago, this was the Mall Hotel with a bar he used to frequent regularly. He sighs, remembering the time he left one night at closing time drunk out of his tree, then jumped in the back of a friend's pickup and berated people on Portage Avenue for the wrongs committed against Native people. And the time Willie Spence invited him to a party when he got his student loan and they woke up the next day in Calgary. He sighs again, then crosses the street to the bus depot.

Removing a key from his pocket, he makes his way to locker 114 and removes his duffle bag. Tattered and green with many baggage claim tickets hanging from its straps, the bag has followed him for thousands of miles since he left the army. He swings it over his shoulder, then leaves the depot out the back way where courier and delivery vehicles madly shuffle. He walks up to Ellice Avenue, then checking an address scrawled on a cigarette package, turns and walks west. He walks slowly, methodically, always observing. He studies the residents of the neighborhood, a mix of Portuguese and Asian immigrants and his own Native people. A volatile neighborhood where warring gangs of teenagers meet in school grounds, and brandishing knives carve holes in one another. Dozens end up in hospital, but the wars carry on, recruitment reaching younger and younger members each year. Racism. Sensing the hate in people's eyes as he walks by, he prepares himself for a sudden surprise. He fondles the handle of the knife he keeps taped to his chest.

At the corner of Ellice and Furby, he turns south and stares down the row of low income houses. He checks the address again, and walks up to number 324, a two storey house with half the windows boarded up and huge cracks in the soiled, white plaster that serves as the shell. He removes the set of keys from his pocket, fumbles with the lock, then walks inside, dumping his duffle bag in the front hall.

Inside, the house seems larger. Though the walls are caked with cobwebs and dust, and scratching sounds of bugs and rodents echo in the bare, cracked walls, the interior looks better than the exterior. The paint on the walls seems new, the woodwork still shines with varnish, and the hardwood floors, though dirty, are intact. The fridge and stove work, both bathrooms seem fine, though the shower head upstairs is badly rusted. There are three bedrooms upstairs and two large rooms in the basement. He returns to the living room and collapses on the couch, an old, plush high-back with sagging springs but serviceable cushions. He likes its deep wine colour and runs his fingers along its smooth surface as he thinks. Beside him, on a crooked end table, sits a telephone. He lifts the receiver and listens for a dial tone. It comes through clearly. From his pocket, he removes a list of names scratched on a crumpled, white sheet of paper, then reaches for the phone and dials. After three rings it's answered. "We've got a house," John says into the mouthpiece. "324 Furby."

John hangs up and makes two more similar calls, then rises and takes his duffle bag up the stairs. He chooses the largest bedroom and unpacks, stuffing his clean, but ragged clothes in a dresser and fixing the single bed with his own sheets. He changes his clothes, then hears a knock at the door. He grabs his knife and quietly moves down the stairs. "Who is it?" he asks in a low, monotone voice.

"Frankie," comes the response.

John opens the door. When Frankie comes in carrying a soiled packsack, he looks around with the eyes of a fussy child. "Another dump," he comments.

"Take your stuff upstairs and pick a room, then come back down," John says.

Frankie thumps up the stairs and down the hall. John walks into the living room and stares out the front window. In a front yard across the street, three children clad in worn, winter wear frolic in the snow. Innocence, John muses. Sometimes he longs for it. Sometimes he despises it. When Frankie thumps back down the stairs, John turns to him and says, "This place is a mess. So you know what we do first."

"Start cleaning," Frankie says. He grumbles, but obeys, filling a pail in the kitchen with hot water. He walks into the living room carrying the pail and two rags. John grabs a rag and joins Frankie in wiping the walls. "It's not a bad place," Frankie says after several minutes. "It's just dirty." He steps away from his work and admires the white patch he's made on the wall. John, scrubbing diligently, doesn't answer. Frankie lets out a breath and resumes the task. "It kinda feels good getting back to work. I was goin' nuts last week. Nothin' to do, always worryin'. It's better like this. I'm never scared when we're all together," Frankie says.

"You should always be a little bit scared," John says. "It'll save your life."

Frankie stops scrubbing and leans back, placing a hand on his hip. With the other, he wipes sweat from his face as he looks up at John curiously. Knowing John isn't looking, he shakes his head and drops the rag noisily into the pail.

"Quiet," John commands. Frankie stops. There is another knock at the door. With knife in hand, John peeks through the window.

When he unlocks the bolt and swings the door open, Tracy bustles in swearing. "Fuck, it's cold out there." She's carrying three large grocery bags. "Another dump, eh?" she comments, walking into the kitchen. "Christ, look at this mess. Everything needs cleaning, the cupboards, the fridge, the walls, the floors. It's a good thing I bought lots of Mr. Clean. Eh Johnny! My suitcase is on the front steps, can you grab it for me?"

John steps into the February cold and snatches Tracy's suitcase, a huge piece of luggage weighing close to sixty pounds. He wonders how the hell she made it here carrying this plus the groceries. She takes it from him inside the front door.

"Separate rooms?" she asks.

"Upstairs, take your pick."

"You're cold, Johnny, real cold," she teases, but before John can answer they both turn and greet the large, burly man, also clad in a rumpled, green parka, who is walking up the sidewalk and onto the porch.

"Cliff," John says. "There's one room left. Upstairs."

When Cliff rejoins them in the kitchen, they divide up the pails of soapy water, the rags, and the mops and set to work, Frankie in the living room, Tracy in the kitchen, Cliff upstairs, and John in the basement. With the four of them working together, the entire house is scrubbed clean in under three hours. The rooms smell of pine and disinfectant. The walls have a luster like new paint. Even the floors seem like new.

"That's all it needed," Tracy chirps. "This place is a regular mansion."

"At least it's out of the way," John says, settling into the living room couch. "Now we can start working towards our next show."

"Were there any hitches during the last show?" Cliff asks.

"Not really," John says. "But we could have used you. Frankie here set off a dozen alarms thinking he could divert attention from us."

"It may have been messy, but we pulled it off," Tracy says proudly. "The cops still got nothing to go on." She's standing beside Frankie and puts her hand on his elbow. "Right?" she asks.

"Right," Frankie says.

John says, "I am worried about one thing."

"What's that?" Cliff asks.

"Frankie stole a cab." When he says this, John puts down the rag he's been wiping his hands with and looks accusingly at Frankie.

"I told ya John, no one saw me takin' it. An' I didn't leave behind no prints. I made sure of that."

"I know, Frankie. But it still worries me."

"Don't worry, Frankie," Tracy says. "John's always worried about everything."

Tracy's words haven't made them feel any better. In silence, they ponder the potential consequences. A jet flies overhead drowning out the steady hum of the furnace. When it passes, Cliff says,

"Well. According to the papers, it was a good show."

"Right," John says. "And now it's time to start preparing for the next one." John leads them into the living room and sits on the wine-colored sofa beside Cliff. He waits for Tracy and Frankie to arrange themselves on the floor. Tracy, he sees, has cut her finger and it's bleeding down the back of her hand. Frankie is hugging his arms over his bent knee and looking at Cliff. When they're all settled, John says, "First step, explosives. We'll be needing a lot less than the menagerie we had at the last show. Simple water gels, or even dynamite will do. Any ideas?"

Cliff says, "I'll check what's around town. There's a lot of industry here and plenty of mines up north that need supplies." He speaks slowly and nods at Tracy as he talks. "We should have plenty to choose from."

"Good," John says. "I'll be building a transmitter this time so we can detonate by radio."

"You'll need caps then," Cliff says.

"Right. Aluminum caps. As soon as I get a list together, Frankie can do the shopping for the transmitter. Tracy, you'll set up one of the basement rooms, you know what I need."

Tracy lists a few items. "A professional tool kit, soldering gun, a good work bench, and oh yeah, wiring and electronics."

"What I need," Cliff says, "is some food."

"We've got plenty of that. And there's a van too," John says, passing Tracy a ring of keys and a parking receipt. "It's in the parkade under Portage Place. Black Ford."

Cliff rises and walks to the fridge as Tracy reaches forward.

"Good," she says. When she takes the keys she turns them over in her hands, then looks at John. "Whoever is behind this operation sure has a lot of money," she says, rising to leave.

Money and smarts, John thinks. He takes out a pad to make the list he'll give Frankie: a high frequency radio transmitter, three receivers, additional antennas, and several minute electrical items. It's a hefty list. Expenses. Tracy's right. There's money behind this operation, though the faces are nameless. So far John's met only a contact. He has an idea who 'The Boss' might be; one of several Native people from the movement who now have money. There are five from Alberta that might be behind it. A.J. Cardinal being the most likely. Oil royalties made him a millionaire several times over. They were together in Cache Creek. A.J. was a radical. There's a few organizations that are suspect. When money from the Feds was plentiful, these organizations had high budgets for salaries and court costs. Using Native lawyers and with a lot of committed people, they all earned high salaries on paper, but in reality, kept only fractions of it. The rest went into a pot for the future when funding would be cut. Yeah, John thinks, there's a lot of money out there, and a lot of people angry enough to use it this way. Smart of them to keep it all in secret, though. If he should ever get nabbed, along with Cliff, Frankie, and Tracy, the boss wouldn't be touched.

When he finishes the list, he passes it to Frankie who runs his eyes down the paper, working his lips over each item he reads; aluminum foil, eight double 'A' batteries, micro transmitters. "Good," Frankie says. "I got it." But he doesn't move from his position on the floor.

"But?" John asks.

Frankie's face contorts in thought. "How come no one knows what we're doin'? I mean, when there's any other bombs, like the IRA or PLO or somethin', everyone knows it's them. But with us, there ain't nothin'. We don't got a name like that."

"Those are questions we shouldn't be asking, Frankie."

"I know, but I was just thinkin'. If somethin' happens to us and we die, people won't know what we're tryin' to do, or why. Seems like it would all be a waste." He looks at John and then drops his eyes to the list in his hands. "But you're right. I shouldn't be thinkin' like this."

"You can't help thinking," says John. He smiles and Frankie smiles back, encouraged by John's open face, the way his eyes seem friendly and warm. So he dares a question.

"How come you're in this John?" he asks. "Tracy's in it for the fun, I'm pretty sure of that. Me and Cliff are in it for the money, but somethin' tells me that for you, there's another reason. It's like, you get real hateful about somethin' whenever a show gets real close."

"Frankie, you amaze me," John says. He smiles again and adds in a voice containing wonder and admiration, "You see truths that fly right over everyone else's head. It's scary."

The smile of a shy kid when he's flattered wraps Frankie's face. "My mom used to say the creator didn't give me much in the head, but he gave me real smart eyes."

John beams. "I like that."

"But I was right, eh? There's a bigger reason for doin' this than just money for you. I always thought there was. But if you don't wanna tell me, I'll understand."

"It's not that," John says. His eyes narrow as he thinks back, forcing himself to remember what lies behind his hatred. Sorrow, he decides, and anger.

"It was personal," he says finally. "Someone I knew got hurt bad and since then whatever I've done has had just one motive. Revenge." He looks at Frankie who's chewing his lower lip, his eyes wide with attention. "It was someone I cared about a lot."

"I understand," Frankie says.

But John doesn't seem to hear him. Lost in memory, the words form themselves as he leans forward. "It was right after Wounded Knee. I was just a kid, but I guess she thought I was old enough to follow her around on the protests and the marches. There was an energy back then, really electric, not for everyone, but for those in the movement. We were organized, we were on the move-at least that's how I remember it. I don't know, maybe I've glorified it now, but that's how it seemed. We were alive as if for the first time. Indians doing things. Defying everybody who'd put us down in the past. You know what I mean? But of course there was death as well as life. Informants. Unknown eyes at gatherings. Then people started going to prison, and in the States, disappearing. There were deaths, murders, executions committed by the F.B.I. I wasn't sure if they were true until..."

"I know," Frankie says softly. He puts his hand out and touches John's arm and John realizes for the first time how big his hand is, the hand of a powerful man who holds his anger back. He sees that Frankie knows things he never suspected he did. So John tells him, his voice barely rising above a whisper, how his life reached a turning point when he was only fifteen and never looked back.

It was after a protest in Kenora, John says, and his mother was hitchhiking with him late at night near the Manitoba border. It was a beautiful night. The kind when the sky is filled with stars. John's mother was telling him their names and pointing out the constellations, like Orion, The Great Bear. She liked Orion, she said, because it reminded her of warriors from an earlier time.

Traffic was sparse, but a car rounded a turn behind them. She automatically turned and thrust her right thumb into the wind. The car slowed down and pulled to a halt in front of them. They hesitated, not sure if they should accept the ride. It was an R.C.M.P. vehicle and there had been a lot of trouble with the R.C.M.P.. When the passenger door opened, an officer boomed, "If you want a ride, get in." They hesitated for a moment then got in. The car drove back onto the dark highway. The officer asked,

"You going home from your Pow Wow?"

"Protest," John's mother corrected.

"Whatever." The cop waved one hand in the air dismissively. A big hand, beefy, and with a ring on the pinky finger like college boys wear. "You know," he added, "some of you Indian women sure are pretty." He put his hand on the seat between him and John's mother. The fingers tapped the upholstery.

"I think you should drop us off," John's mother said.

"Hell, I'm not going to do that. You wanted a ride, so I'm going to give you a ride," the cop said. He smiled and placed his hand on her shoulder. John's mother stiffened at his touch.

"Let us out, please."

But the cop drove on. He kept his hand on her shoulder, and when they came to a curve in the road he moved his hand down to her thigh. John looked out the window. The telephone poles were flying past and the dark forest seemed a blur. They came to a side road and the cop wheeled down it and brought the car to a stop. "Tell the kid to get out," he said. "Go for a walk or something." He nodded towards John, then grabbed her by the shoulders. John grabbed the door handle, but it wouldn't open. Frantically he struggled with it, but it wouldn't budge. He looked into the front and saw only the cop. His mother was somewhere beneath. As the cop looked into the back to see if John was still there, John's mother grabbed for his revolver, but was unable to get it out of its holster. The cop felt her tugging and turned his attention back to her. She grabbed a flashlight on the floor and struck at him blindly. She hit his shoulder first, and then as he wheeled in surprise, his head, once, then twice, bringing blood from his forehead and nose. The cop howled and John's mother pushed open the door. She wrenched the back door open to let John out and together, they ran for the woods. But the cop wasn't through. He stumbled out of the car and ran after them. When he was closing in, John's mother told John to keep running, then she stopped, turned, and faced the cop. He threw her violently to the ground and their bodies rolled about in the dark, legs, arms, heads. John heard punches. He heard his mother scream. She cried out once long and loud.

From the woods where he'd stopped John heard the muffled sobs of his mother and the cop grunting as if lifting a heavy sack. Then his breathing became guttural and rhythmic. John felt sick. He put his forehead against the bark of a tree and vomited on his shoes. He could hear the cop breathing heavily and scrabbling around in the undergrowth, but he couldn't hear his mother. Not one sound. John waited until he heard the cop's receding sounds in the bush and the sudden start of the car's engine. When he ventured back into the clearing he found his mother curled into a ball like a child sleeping. Her shirt was torn. Her jeans were lying a few feet away, bloody and soiled. He knelt over her and felt her skin turning cold. His mother was dead. John listened to his heart beating, the rage building in his chest like a bomb waiting to explode. He lifted his head, hatred burning in his eyes as he branded the cop's face in his memory.

* * *

Wayne sits in a restaurant on Princess Street eating lunch. A friend, Jim Munroe, a few years older than Wayne, sits across from him. It is too early for the lunchtime crowd, so the restaurant is quiet. Wayne and Jim speak little while they eat, and with their meals finished, sit back using their tongues to pick at their teeth. "I'm sorry pal, there isn't much more I can tell you," Jim says. "I've heard the place might have been bombed by someone Native, but that's all I know."

"If it was a local you'd know about it?" Wayne asks. It seems to him that Jim knows more than he's saying. He keeps shifting his eyes to his empty plate.

"Our community is pretty small and the grapevines slick. I'd know, unless it was someone new, or from out of province." Jim was part of the movement in the sixties and seventies, and even now, tied down with a civic job, has managed to keep pace with things. He adds, "I saw that film you guys did last year about Anna Mae Aquash. I liked it. Now I hear you've just finished another one." When Jim changes the topic, Wayne goes along, biding his time.

"That might be our last," he says. "From now on,

it could all be video."

"Uhuh. That seems to be the trend. Film is almost obsolete."

"You still need a good camera team though. If we had one on the film we just shot, it would have looked a lot better. You need the proper ingredients, just like anything. If the script wasn't so tight, we would have been in a lot of trouble."

"Well, trouble is what we're good at," Jim smiles.

"So you don't think there's anything to these bombings?"

"I really don't know. I haven't heard anything, but if I had, others would have too, then in a few days, everyone would know it."

"Do you think it's possible?"

Jim takes his napkin and idly folds it. "Anything is possible, but it would have to be a damn secret operation and it would need a lot of money behind it. This is terrorism you're talking about."

"There's been a lot of talk over the years and there's a lot of rich Native people now," Wayne says.

"Yeah, talk. But think of what it would take to pull a stunt like this. The money to throw away, the people to do the jobs, they'd have to be either very committed or crazy, probably both."

"You sound like an authority on the subject," Wayne says, smiling. "Paint a picture for me."

Jim grabs a toothpick and pokes at his teeth, then shrugs. "Logically speaking, you'd need a group of people, maybe five, who before taking this on were very low profile. They'd have to be trained in handling and designing explosives, either through industry or the military. They'd also have to know how to break in and out of places without getting caught, and to always keep their mouths shut, and have enough balls to do it. Imagine the risk they're taking, the anxiety that would go with it," he says, shaking his head. "Then there's the hierarchy. There'd have to be someone at the top for direction and money, plus a middleman to keep the hierarchy safe in case the group gets caught. It would have to be so underground that they could live next door to you without you noticing anything out of the ordinary."

Wayne's hand strokes his upper lip. "So could Native people be behind it?"

"Sure, but that doesn't mean they are. It could be the Ku Klux Klan trying to paint Native people red with bad publicity."

"Wouldn't they be more sensationalist?"

"Subtlety is more effective. But it could be Native people. Heard from your brother lately?"

"He was in town for a week. It was good to see him. Usually, he's never in one place long enough to establish a fixed address."

"Where's he off to now?"

"West somewhere. Suppose I won't see him for another year." Jim suddenly lifts his toothpick from his mouth and waves it at Wayne.

"See, if it's a group of Native people, your brother would be an ideal candidate. Moving around a lot, a low profile, once a dynamic member of the movement, and he's been in the army."

"Eh," Wayne snorts, "my brother's no terrorist."

"I'm not saying he is, only that he'd be a prime candidate if someone started looking. But of course there are thousands like him. Is he still involved with your radical buddies?"

"Naw, he picks up odd jobs here and there. He's a drifter."

"Well," Jim says, out the corner of his mouth. "He's always had a major chip on his shoulder."

"Quit it," Wayne grumbles, unsure whether he should find this amusing or alarming.

"All right," Jim says, sitting back. "But you see what I mean."

"I get the point," Wayne says, indignantly, then changes the subject. "So what else is new around town?"

"There's a protest in a couple of weeks at Indian Affairs about the new bill the minister is trying to railroad through the house. He'll be in town that day."

"Yeah, I'll probably be there. A follow-up for an interview my boss is doing with him."

"Mmm," Jim mumbles, checking his watch. "I have to get back to work. Come by the office sometime and say hello, even if you don't need information."

Wayne smiles. Then asks, "But if you do hear something, you'll let me know?"

"You bet," Jim says, smiling back. He turns and heads for the exit.

Wayne takes a sip of water and broods. In a week and a half of digging, he's established some facts that suggest the bombings are linked, but nothing to support his theory of Native involvement. Maybe it isn't a Native group, he thinks, but what would the motive be then? What Jim said? To discredit Native people in the public's eye? No, the public holds Native people in enough discredit. They don't need any more help, particularly something as risky as this. The motive would have to be powerful, something worth giving up life for. The targets themselves are enough, it seems, to point the finger at Native people. Alcohol, the church, and The Hudson's Bay Company. What else would those three have in common? And yet it seems too tidy. He's lost in these thoughts when a woman suddenly sits across from him. Wayne knows her; Elsie Moore, a member of the Native Communications Network's board of directors.

"Hello, Wayne," she says, smiling so that the gap between her two front teeth shows prominently. Wayne nods. He's not too friendly with board members.

"I hear you're working on quite a story." Oh boy, Wayne thinks, here we go. He looks away and when he doesn't speak, Elsie adds, "I'm not one for cheap gossip, Wayne, but I wonder about your motives here. I wonder if it's in our best interest to blab this around."

"No one's blabbing anything yet," Wayne says.

"I wouldn't want you or anyone in your family being the target of a scandal. This thing would make the public paranoid. There's no telling who might be under attack from vigilantes. There are a lot of people with pasts in the movement," she says, "a lot of people. We might have to let you go for your own protection. If word about this gets out, it might seem like we're involved. It's terrorism, we don't need that, no matter how valiant it seems."

"Obviously there's angry people out there," Wayne says. "What they're doing is wrong, but they're angry for a reason. This is probably the only way they see how to strike back. That takes guts."

"So you support them?"

"No," Wayne snaps. "But I'm a journalist. I want to find out about them."

"Your curiosity is dangerous, Wayne," she says, gravely.

"How did you find out?" Wayne asks

"This is a small community, word spreads fast," she replies, pausing to light a cigarette. "I like your work Wayne. All I'm saying is think before you become too involved. You might learn too much, then you'd be a danger, to all of us. You'd be a valuable person to lose."

"Are you speaking for the board?" Wayne asks.

"I'm speaking as a member of the board," she answers, standing up. "It's been nice talking to you. Bye, bye."

* * *

Wayne sits at his desk tapping a pencil against the phone with the receiver pressed between his shoulder and cheek. He's on hold waiting for information from a friend on the police force. His anticipation beats the silence on the line as his hopes rise with optimism one second, and fall into doubt the next. The silence ends with a click as his friend, Sergeant Ray Jeffries, comes back on the line. "This might be what you're looking for," Ray says. "A mining distributor reported a case of dynamite and blasting caps stolen last weekend."

"That's it," Wayne says, flipping his pencil into the air. It lands on the desk and bounces to the floor. "Thanks a lot Ray, I owe you another lunch."

"Sure," Ray replies, adding this promise to six others. "What do you need this for anyhow?"

"I wish I could tell you," Wayne says, "but we're trying to keep a lid on it."

"Right."

Wayne hangs up and leans back into the chair drumming his fingers on the arm rest. Brooding over the facts he's pieced together, he tries to form a picture in his head when Janet pokes hers into the office.

"Mind if I have a seat?" she asks. He motions for her to sit down. She does, then asks, "How do you handle racists?"

Wayne shrugs. "I ignore them."

Janet nods. "I'm still caught up in this anger phase. I had a few words with our minister. What a racist creep. You expect more from a cop."

"A cop?"

"An ex-cop." Janet lights a cigarette and flips back her hair. The fluorescent lighting filters through the black and highlights the red. "What did he say about the Federation?"

"He's cagey on that subject. Full of talk about fiscal responsibility and commitment. He wants to see them go under real bad, I could feel it."

"He's cagey on all subjects. I think he'd like the department to take control of all the Federation's programs."

"And the fine print in that bill he's proposing might give him the power," she says, shaking her head.

"Don't you love white politicians who still think we can't run our lives?" Wayne asks, his voice peppered in sarcasm.

"They don't understand the difference in our values," she says.

"They know there's a difference," Wayne says, "but they don't give a shit. They want us to fit the Native mold they've created for us."

"We're still, 'the Native problem', as far as they're concerned." Janet grabs a handful of her hair and examines it. Then asks, "How's the bomb story happening?"

"I'm making progress, but I meant to ask you. How many people know about this thing?"

"You and I, as far as I know."

"Not members of the board? Not Elsie Moore?"

Janet's head snaps to Wayne's, her eyes wide. Then she relaxes again and leans back. In the past Elsie, a conservative, and Janet, a believer in the new movement, have had battles over NCN's paper and magazine and their content and angle. "What did you tell her?" she asks.

"I told her I had been working on the story for a few days and that I would continue working on it. I told her to mind her own business."

"So what have you really got?"

"That there was a theft of explosives at the St. Jean military base south of Montreal three weeks before the first bombing."

"And?"

"The explosives taken matched those used in the Montreal and Toronto blasts. Then a week later, explosives were stolen from a manufacturing plant in Sudbury."

"This is what, a month before the blast here?"

"Three weeks actually. The theft in Sudbury was a big one, they took enough explosives to do the job on The Bay, and the type matches again. The cops are sure now that the bombings are related."

"And the Native connection?"

"The motive is the only link so far." Wayne leans forward and looks at his notes, his elbows resting on the desk and his thumbs pressing into his forehead. "The cops have to see the connection, but with all the tension between them and the Native community, I'd say they're afraid to speculate publicly."

"What about within the community itself. Any word?"

"No one knows, or at least no one's saying anything. It's possible, and if it's true, the feeling is it will stay miles underground. They won't be uncovered by police investigation, they'll be uncovered by our own people. Word of mouth, something like that. But so far, no word, and no proof."

"Do you have anything else?"

"Just all the mundane facts about how the jobs were done. They break and enter in the night and plant the charges. They've been using timers, having several charges located in strategic points going off at once. There was also another theft. Three days ago, a mining distributor reported dynamite and blasting caps stolen from its warehouse."

"So there's going to be another blast."

"It appears that way. Where, we have no way of knowing."

"Some place west?"

"And soon if I guess right. The previous bombings have followed each other at five-week intervals. And the Bay was bombed a month ago. The explosives just stolen aren't nearly as large or as destructive a lot as they needed for The Bay, but it's enough to do damage wherever they so choose, assuming it's them behind the theft."

"Where do you think they'll strike?" Janet asks.

Wayne's eyebrows curl and his body shivers. It's a funny feeling, he thinks, predicting where a bomb will go off next. Do they have a responsibility to warn or do they wait and report? "Well, they've hit a Catholic church, a brewery, and The Hudson's Bay. I suppose the R.C.M.P. is a logical target. Or Indian Affairs."

"What about the legislatures? They're starting a new session in Edmonton."

"Maybe," Wayne says, "but I like Regina better. Louis Riel and all that stuff. It would be a logical place to make a statement. Maybe the Indians and the Metis are united in this one."

"That's just it, there have been no statements. No one has claimed responsibility. Other than the targets, there's nothing to suggest anyone Native is even involved."

Wayne's phone buzzes. He answers then passes it to Janet. "It's for you," he tells her. Janet grabs the phone as Wayne leans back in his chair and stares out the window at the waning winter. It has to be Native people, he thinks. The church, alcohol, Hudson's Bay and the fur trade; it's so obvious. He scratches his chin slowly. Maybe it's too obvious.

When Janet puts the phone down she says to Wayne, "There's a press conference at the cop shop. You'd better come with me."

* * *

John Weenusk sits in a once elegant restaurant studying the menu: New York steak, breaded veal, assorted burgers. Across from him is a woman in her mid-forties. Her dark hair is curled up in a bun and tinted prescription glasses rest on her high cheek bones. He knows her name as Betty, but also knows it isn't her real name. He thinks she's Ojibway. For the past several months, she's been his boss. He nips at his salad calmly, but as always, is guarded and calculating.

"Is everything set?" asks the woman.

"We're set," John says, lifting a fork to his mouth. "All we need is a time and a target."

The woman nods. "The time is soon. The target will be here, in Winnipeg."

This news catches John off guard. "Isn't this breaking our pattern?"

"Yes," she says, smiling so that John sees the gap between her two front teeth. She enjoys making him uncomfortable. "But with the publicity we'll be getting in the next few days, breaking the pattern will work in our favour." She waves her hand in the air when John looks like he's going to ask about this publicity and adds, "Don't worry, we're not shooting in the dark. We're following a plan that's been set for a long time. So all you have to do is keep out of sight for the next little while."

"But..."

"No buts. The target is set and so is the time."

"We need to know a few things. We need-"

"You need to be ready when we call you. But in the meantime, don't be alarmed by what you hear or read."

"Are things going to get dirty?"

"Messy, but not dirty." She stands, dropping two twenties on the table and says, "I have to go. Stay and finish your meal. You'll hear from me soon."

John watches her walk to the door, then dips his fork into his Greek salad, searching for sparse chunks of feta. She stops at the front counter and opens her handbag. From it she takes a notebook and reads from a page in the middle, then stuffs it back into the handbag. John chews thoughtfully on leaves of romano lettuce. He waits to the count of twenty after she's closed the door, then he rises and follows.

* * *

Elsie Moore crosses Portage Avenue and enters the Kensington building, a tall, mirrored glass structure housing several government departments. The seventeenth floor is occupied by Indian and Northern Affairs. She rides the elevator to the seventeenth floor, then steps out and strides past many cubicles before stopping at an office door. She knocks, then enters.

"Have a seat," a middle-aged man says. And then, "Are our terrorists set?"

"They have their instructions."

"Good," says the man, "the story should be breaking within the next hour or so. If everything goes according to plan, we'll be laughing."

* * *

Across the street, John Weenusk sits on a bus stop bench. His mind is awhirl. He followed Betty down Spence street and then along the sidewalk for eight blocks east. At one point it looked as if she might hail a cab. She walked on and straight to Indian Affairs. But how can this be? Maybe he confused two women of the same height and was headed off in a totally meaningless direction. But that can't be either, because he was following her turquoise jacket. He saw no one else wearing one like it. John glances up at the towering building. Perhaps there are other departments she could have gone into. He knows this is very unlikely, but it's a possibility. He looks up and down Smith Street. It's a cold afternoon, the snowplows rumble down sidewalks as pedestrians duck into doorways for safety.

John feels his face freezing. He walks through the streets practicing a measured calm and heads home.

* * *

Among the living room furnishings, there is now a television. Purchased at Tracy's insistence, its function is to help pass time as the crew awaits instructions for the next show. As John enters the living room he sees that everyone is gathered around. An air of excitement fills the room. The TV news at six begins with an item from the public safety building. A heavy-set policeman is nervously reading a prepared statement. "Though we've suspected, in cooperation with the R.C.M.P., that the bombings were in fact related, it wasn't until today that this new information came forward. We received a written document from a group called 'ARM' claiming responsibility for the bombing of the downtown Hudson's Bay building in Winnipeg last month, the Labatt's Brewery in Toronto last December, and the St. Jean's Basilica in Montreal last November. The group describes itself as a Native terrorist group. It is this department's belief, and that of the R.C.M.P., that this claim is legitimate." When Cliff turns the television off, the room is silent. Tracy is sitting on the floor with her arms wrapped around her knees rocking back and forth in thought. John is thinking about his earlier conversation with Betty, understanding now what she meant by publicity.

The first person to speak is Frankie. "We have a name," he says in a proud whisper. "ARM."

"Was this supposed to happen?" Cliff asks, directing the question at John. His voice rises, indicating surprise. When John nods, Cliff asks, "Then where does this put us?"

"In the public eye," Tracy answers. "We've been given notoriety."

"Well," Cliff says. "I'm not sure I want to be notorious."

"ARM," Frankie says. "What do you suppose it means? 'Something' Resistance Movement?"

"I like it," Tracy says. "It sounds strong and catchy."

"And enough like AIM to connect us to the movement twenty-five years ago," Cliff says, his arms dropping to his side as he leans back in his chair. "So what do we terrorists do now?"

John strokes his chin before answering. "Our next show will happen soon, and it will be here in Winnipeg," he says. "Until then, we sit tight."

"At least now we have a cause," Tracy says.

"At least now we have a name," Frankie adds.

John is in thought. His eyebrows are curled as he remembers Betty walking to Indian Affairs after lunch. It weighs on him like a lead block.

* * *

Wayne is in his office doing another column at Janet's request. He reads what he's just written: *As a result of ARM's actions, Native people must prepare for a conservative backlash.*

He sits back and scans the article. Since ARM's proclamation seven days ago, he's received phone calls from government ministers and several from outraged members of the non-Native community. But he knew it was coming. Give them any reason and the right wing will try and undo the progress of any oppressed people. Wayne wonders how the conservative Chiefs in the confederation are reacting. Probably ready to pull the plug just as quick as the rest of the right. When he looks up, Janet is standing in front of his desk. "You look self-satisfied. Must come from being a media-star."

When the news story broke, Wayne did an item for NCN's television news team. It was seen coast to coast and other radio and television stations have been calling for interviews everyday since. "Lucky timing, that's all." Wayne leans to his computer and punches a command. The laser printer jumps in with a low hum.

"Well," Janet says. "It turned out super, for us and for you. We might not be able to afford to keep you here."

Wayne looks up from the printer to see if Janet is serious. Maybe she's heard that C.B.C. called.

* * *

For the group labelled ARM, time seems frozen. But when the telephone rings and heads spin, there is a sense that the long wait may finally be over. It rings a second time. The group stares at the phone dumbly. On the third ring Tracy wails, "Answer it, Johnny."

John reaches over and picks up the receiver.

A voice says simply, "The target is Indian Affairs, the seventeenth floor of the Kensington building. Tomorrow at noon. There is going to be a demonstration. Enter the building, then do the operation, and blend back in with the crowd, but make sure the place blows after midnight."

John leaves a long silence, listening to the breathing on the other end of the line. He wonders if it's Betty he's listening to. The voice is like hers, but she's obviously trying to disguise it, making it sound guttural. He finally asks, "And then what?"

"Do not return to the house. Once the demonstration ends, you'll be given your final payment. After that, it's over. Do you understand?"

"Over?" John says. His head rises sharply, meeting Tracy's inquiring eyes. He wheels and looks out the window. Over, he thinks. The word turns in his mind. He always knew it would end, yet it's still a shock. Perhaps a part of him believed it would never end.

"Yes, over. Good luck."

When John puts the receiver down, he meets three sets of inquiring eyes.

"Well?" Tracy demands.

"The show is tomorrow."

"What's the target?" asks Cliff.

"Indian Affairs," John answers quietly, "noon, though the blast has to be after midnight."

"Indian Affairs," Cliff says. "I like that."

Frankie asks, "And then?"

"That's it," John says.

"There won't be another show?" Frankie's eyes bug out and his jaw drops. John shakes his head.

"Why not?" Tracy asks. "Because of the slip-up at the last show? They don't think we can do it properly anymore?"

"Maybe someone's onto us," Cliff wonders aloud. "The R.C.M.P., or C.S.I.S."

Tracy asks accusingly, "Is there something you haven't been telling us, Johnny?"

John leans forward, trying to figure out a reason that sounds plausible. Frankly, he doesn't know either. "Up to now, each show has been a symbolic act. We've destroyed three symbols of oppression against Native people without any loss of life. This last show will be against the government itself, a final statement. Our point will be made," he says, almost believing it himself. "There's no reason to continue. We stop now while we still have our freedom."

The room is silent until Cliff speaks.

"Well, lets make sure we do this one right," he says. "Then we can retire."

* * *

Alone together in bed, John and Tracy lie on their backs and stare at the ceiling. Lights from the street reflect on the walls of the bare room. Somewhere a tap is dripping.

"This will be the last time, won't it?" Tracy asks.

"You knew it would come to this."

"I know, but... why always just before a show or

just after? I can teach you to love, John. I can reach whatever it is in there that hurts you so much. You just have to let me."

John lies still, thinking back over the months they have been together. Her warm flesh is nuzzled against his and it feels good, but something isn't right. He wonders what. It isn't her, or them. It's the next show, and it nags at him. Indian Affairs, where he watched his contact, Betty, enter days before. Maybe she was casing the place out. But that's their job. It puzzles and worries him. Something isn't right.

Knowing he won't let her in, Tracy asks, "So what will you do now?" When he doesn't answer, she says, "You're a cold, crazy bastard, Johnny, but I love you, I really do." He finally turns to her. There is something new in his eyes as he reaches to her, something vulnerable. Tracy sees it, but knows this is as close as they will ever get. She accepts his advance and they melt together. Their sex is intense, painful. When it's done, she falls asleep.

John lies in bed. Nervous, he gets up and goes down stairs where Cliff and Frankie are packing up the equipment. He smokes a cigarette and looks out the window. After a while he says, "We're moving out." When Cliff and Frankie give him strange looks, he simply says he feels uneasy. He tells them to wake up Tracy and get the stuff in the van. He's taking them to a motel.

"It's all ready," says Cliff, placing a suitcase at John's feet. "These are the leftovers." John stares at the suitcase for a moment, then grabs it.

"This we have to get rid of. I'll do it right away. Have everything packed by the time I get back, and make sure Tracy gets up. I shouldn't be more than an hour."

John steps out of the house into the cold night. Normally he'd give a task like this to Cliff or Frankie, but John wants some time alone to collect his thoughts. He places the suitcase in the back of the van, then gets in the front and pulls away from the curb. It is dark out. He sees that several street lamps are out. His headlights bounce off the street and reflect against the trees. He feels the van's engine struggle and pulls off to the side to let it warm up. He shuts off the lights and sits listening to the motor's hum.

In the distance is Ellice Avenue. He watches traffic and spots a pair of Native boys walking along the sidewalk shivering in their light leather jackets. They're about twelve or thirteen, he thinks. Perhaps brothers. He remembers when he was that age. Young and angry. He remembers Wayne coming home from school with a bloody nose, crying. He was in a fight and won. But the pain he felt wasn't from the punches. It was from his opponent's words. Racist words: boggin, wagon burner, welfare Indian. Wayne cried in his mother's arms, and John cried tears of anger. He wipes a lone tear from his cheek and breathes harshly. He's answering that anger, he thinks, right or wrong.

The motor is idling well now. He puts it in gear and checks the side mirror for traffic. In the distance, he sees a number of cars pull up in front of the house he just left. There are three black and white cars of the city police, two R.C.M.P. vehicles, and four unmarked sedans. Their doors open and a dozen or more men swarm the house. John's pulse thunders. He watches lights in the house go on and off and jumps when he hears the sickening crack of automatic weapons. Fighting panic, he slams the gas pedal and the van peels away, fishtailing onto Ellice Avenue.

Cruising down Ellice and its sparse, two a.m. traffic, his mind races. Priority number one, dump the van. Crossing Donald Street, he turns down a dark alley poring over the possibilities. Did the cops track them down? Were they tipped off? Either way, he supposes, it doesn't matter. Some slip-up, some betrayal has ended ARM's brief existence and left him on a wire. Now, he can see only one path to follow.

* * *

It is a night of phone calls. The ringing jars Wayne and Theresa from dreams to early morning darkness. Momentarily uncertain why they are awake, the second ring bolts them to alertness. Theresa reaches for the phone. "Hello?" she mumbles. She passes the receiver to Wayne. "It's for you." Wayne grabs at it in the dark, then tucks it between his head and pillow.

"It's five in the morning," he mutters.

"Sorry to wake you up," Janet's voice says, bright and cheery. "But it's important." She takes a breath and then says, "Three hours ago, the R.C.M.P. raided a house on Furby Street. They found our terrorists."

"Ours?"

"ARM, they killed two and have one in custody, but they're being tight-lipped about it. They won't release names or information. No one can even get a picture of the guy in custody. But they let it slip that a fourth one got away. Apparently, he'd gone out just before the Mounties arrived. That's all there is for now, but the story's in the open and our board be damned, we're gonna have the best coverage."

Wayne is sitting up wide-eyed and alert. "It won't be finished until the fourth is caught, but this is the breaker. What do you want me to do?"

"What do you think?"

"I think five is too early for even an eager superstar reporter."

"See you in an hour."

* * *

In the shower, Wayne wonders how the R.C.M.P. found the terrorists. Maybe, he thinks, someone somewhere let something slip. Loose tongues. Or maybe they were too sloppy at the last bombing. Something could have been left behind that the cops followed up on. Perhaps the group wasn't all that professional after all. It's not surprising that they were caught. They were at the top of the country's most wanted list. The manhunt, though well camouflaged, must have been immense. C.S.I.S. must have been involved. He rinses, shaves, brushes his teeth, and slips back into the bedroom to dress. Theresa is asleep again, her lips jutting out beneath her long, flowing hair.

Maybe he will do a story for the paper, Wayne thinks, putting on underwear. Headlines run through his head. *ONE ARM CAUGHT, TWO ARMS DEAD, ONE ARM LOOSE*, it would read. Or maybe, *TERRORISTS DEAD AT ARMS END*. When he's fully clothed, he goes downstairs and puts the coffee on, then pops a few vitamins. The past few days he's been ridden with stress and he needs to settle himself down. He focuses on the coffee machine's drip and employs a breathing exercise, learned years before at a seminar on meditation, by saying the word "Zuma" over and over again. The exercise works. Wayne feels his heartbeat slowing. He has to be calm, he thinks, when lives are at stake. Alert to details. As the thought runs through his brain, a detail catches his eye. Under the kitchen table is an air vent. When the basement light is on, the light shines through the vent, and on this morning, light is refracted throughout the kitchen. Wayne finds this puzzling. He's sure he turned the basement lights off. He studies the vent as he rinses a coffee cup. When the light in the basement suddenly goes out, Wayne's puzzlement becomes fear. He pulls a knife from the drawer and moves to the basement door. The thumping of footsteps is clearly audible. Wayne's grip on the knife tightens as the door swings open. His brother John comes out of the stairwell.

"Jesus," Wayne says, "that's twice in a month you've nearly scared me to death."

"I needed a place to stay," John says. He walks over to the counter and turns on the radio, then sniffs at the finished coffee. "Can I have a cup?" he asks, reaching into the cupboard for a mug.

Wayne watches his brother closely, his eyes narrowed. John grabs a mug and it clashes with others on the shelf. He crosses the kitchen to the coffee machine, keeping his back to Wayne the whole time. Wayne's eyes narrow further, then grow cold as the silence becomes tense.

As John pours, the morning news comes on. The lead story is about ARM.

"One ARM is caught, two ARMS are dead, and one ARM is loose say the R.C.M.P. following an early morning raid..."

With the two mugs full, John freezes, at first listening intensely and then turning his eyes to Wayne's. Wayne recognizes something in them he hasn't seen in years. Hatred; a remote, cold anger that seems to glaze over John's eyes. "You know something about that?" Wayne asks. He's still holding the knife, and suddenly it feels comfortable in his grip. John passes him a mug of coffee. It feels hot in Wayne's hand, as hot as his cheeks. He says, "They're talking about you, aren't they?"

John remains silent swallowing first one, then two gulps of coffee, but in his eyes Wayne sees a hint of an answer. Those eyes. He saw the same look in them years ago when a lodge owner's son called John a "buck" and John knocked him off the dock and into the frigid water at Caribou Lake. He saw it, too, the night John came home from the occupation of Anishnabe Park and told him their mother had left. A cold look, both focussed and abstract. "You won't need the knife,"

John finally says. Wayne releases it and the knife falls to the floor. "But you will need that," John says. He points to the coffee mug.

Blindly Wayne throws the mug at John's head and it shatters against the far cupboard where it runs down the wall and into a puddle on the floor. Wayne glares at John, overcome with fury as his blood pounds the walls of his skull. He wheels and walks in a restrained step from the kitchen and slumps onto the sofa.

In a few minutes John comes into the room carrying a suitcase. "I was hoping," he says, "to be gone by the time you woke up."

"You've got nowhere to go," Wayne states.

"Maybe not, but I can't stay here."

"Do you have any idea what the fuck you're into?" Wayne can see as soon as he's asked it that John knows exactly what he's into. And has been into for some time now. When he shrugs, Wayne says in a calm voice, "I can't believe this." He shakes his head. "For weeks I've been busting my ass on a story about Native terrorism that no one would believe. And now I find out I've been on the trail of my own brother."

"Wayne, look, I didn't want you to find out this way."

"Oh? What were you hoping? That I'd be sitting at a press conference and the R.C.M.P. would approach me and tell me the fourth terrorist was my brother, any idea where we can find him? Or better yet, maybe Jason or Jessica could hear your name on television. What if you were blown away, how do you expect us to take this kind of news?"

"I haven't thought about it very much."

"I'll bet there's a ton of shit you haven't thought about very much."

"And there's a ton of shit you know nothing about." John turns his back on Wayne, struggling to control himself, then says, "I'm sorry this is causing you so much pain, but two people close to me are dead and I have to keep running. Right now, I'm not very worried about what other people will think. What's done is done."

"Beautiful, that makes me feel a whole lot better."

"This is pointless," John says, "I have to go."

"Your ass is burnt, it's finished," Wayne says. From behind he can see that John's pant leg is ripped. A blood stain is forming near his knee. "All you're gonna do is get yourself killed."

"I have one more job to do."

"Job?" Wayne stares at him. "It's over."

"No, it's not," John states, his voice as sharp edged as an axe. He returns Wayne's stare and then sits on the sofa. "What I'm about to say is going to freak you right out of your comfortable family paradise, little brother." John waves his hand in the air, indicating the T.V., the Morriseau prints on the walls, the wall to wall carpeting they had installed last fall. "What I'm going to tell you has to do with your family, about the mother you thought ran away."

* * *

The news of ARM's demise spreads fast, and the

switch board at the Native Communications Network is swamped by calls from press agencies worldwide.

Janet's own phone buzzes and she answers. Yet another call for Wayne. She explains quickly that he hasn't come in yet. When the voice on the other end of the line rumbles on, her mind drifts. Where the hell is Wayne? He's four hours late. When the caller hangs up, she buzzes her secretary to try his house one more time. Perhaps he's out following a lead she doesn't know about. Perhaps he went straight to the house on Furby. Her secretary buzzes back. "I just got a phone call. The guy wouldn't leave his name, but it sounded a lot like our missing reporter."

"Where is he, what did he say?"

"He didn't say where he was, but he said ARM's next target was Indian Affairs. He said you should be at today's demonstration."

* * *

At ten-thirty, Janet is out on Portage Avenue in front of Indian Affairs. It's a damp morning with a high, prairie sky overhead, but Native people in large numbers mill around carrying placards. One reads "Self Determination Not For Sale." Another, "Squash Jameson and Bad Bill." On a corner, Janet spots Jim Munroe. He isn't carrying a placard, but passes out buttons promoting self determination. He waves at Janet and when she comes up he asks, "Where's the superstar?"

"You got me. I was hoping you'd heard from

him."

"Nope," Jim states, shaking his head. "Been too busy. But I can give you a scoop."

"What?"

"The Federation denounced our demonstration."

"Typical." Janet shakes her head. "There's plenty of assholes in our national leadership, but no balls."

"If they had balls, they'd be dangerous," Jim says, turning to hand out more buttons.

Janet filters into the growing crowd, eyeing the police assigned to maintain peace. They're watching the crowd which is being swelled by busloads of arrivals from reserves. Five hundred people maybe, Janet guesses. The surprisingly mild weather of early March shines like a smile on the dreary slush being splashed from passing cars. When a cop gets splattered and curses vehemently, Janet chuckles, but she expects the morale of the cops is low. It is still a fact that cops don't like Indians and Indians still mistrust cops, despite the weak efforts of the city counsellors to ease the tension.

From all parts of the city and the reserves around the city, Native people pour onto the corner of Smith and Portage. More placards come out: "Get Jameson Out of Indian Affairs," "Red Power is Back." A sense of community spirit is developing. Faces are cheerful, but determined. An old man wearing a buckskin jacket walks between two teenagers in black leather jackets and punk haircuts. It is a social event where acquaintances are renewed, and a political event where people are united. Janet scans the crowd, then turns to the steel and glass structure above. From within the building, two faces stare at the gathering below. Janet recognizes the Minister's face. This protest could stall the bill that might finally succeed where so many others have failed. To finally wipe out Native rights by giving back control of Native people to Indian Affairs, and then phasing out the department like the government has promised to do. Native people would be high and dry with nothing to show for relinquishing ownership of the land a hundred years and more earlier. Two windows down stands a tall, Native man in a green parka: for him the protest is a welcome distraction from his own covert actions.

* * *

John closes the door slowly behind him and stands with his hands on his hips. When the Minister looks up and reaches for his phone in alarm, John states coolly, "I wouldn't do that if I were you." He undoes his parka. "Mr. Jameson, inside my parka I have explosives connected to a detonator which can be set off by radio wave. In my hand is a small transistor. If it leaves my hand or if I am knocked down, shot, or molested in anyway, the explosives will be detonated. Do you understand?"

The Minister says as coolly, "How did you get in here?" John shakes his head, then opens his coat wide. Lining the inner walls of the parka are two sticks of dynamite. Jameson's eyes shift from the dynamite to John's eyes. "Do you know what the penalty is for threatening an official of the crown?"

"I've already blown up a church, a brewery, and a department store," John says. "I'm not too worried about a white-haired old man."

"So," the Minister says, placing the phone back on the hook. "You're the fourth member of ARM. I thought your style was different. I didn't think you went in for killing."

"It's time for the style to change."

"So you're going to blow us both up?"

"I don't know yet. We have a lot to talk about, but first, I want you to get all your aides and all the staff of this department off the floor and out of the building. Tell them the demonstrators might try to occupy the offices, so to avoid any conflict, everyone can take the afternoon off. Do it now."

Jameson nods. He picks up his phone and buzzes another office. "Pete? Cyrus here. Look, this demonstration thing might get a little heated, so I want you to clear everyone out of the office. Give them the afternoon off. And that goes for you too." He pauses, listening, then says, "No, I'll be staying here for a little while yet. That's it." After he hangs up he raises his eyes to John and asks, "Now what?"

"Phone the R.C.M.P.. Tell them you're being held hostage by a man with enough dynamite to demolish this entire floor."

"Is that a good idea?"

"It's as good an idea as yours. See, I know the R.C.M.P. are right now hearing from the aide you just talked to, so they might as well hear it from you, too. I've studied you, man, you don't have an aide named

Pete. You don't have kids, you were born in Thunder Bay, and you worked for the R.C.M.P. while you were in law school. I know all about you." When Jameson turns to pick up the phone, John adds, "You better warn them about the transmitter and how I've wired this thing. You wouldn't want a sniper to shoot me."

Jameson nods. When he dials the R.C.M.P. number his hand trembles, but he stays in a firm, clear voice,

"Five minutes and they'll be in position to take you down. If you want to reconsider, this is the time to do it."

As Jameson makes the call, John slides to one side of the window. Outside, the demonstration is about to begin and the crowd has swelled to thousands. City police struggle to contain them within traffic barriers blocking Smith Street and part of Portage Avenue. The partitioned area becomes an urban reserve, larger in number than many others.

John's eyes shift from the crowd to the parkade across the street, then up at the Delta Hotel on Portage. He wonders where he will see them first.

Jameson hangs up and turns to John. "What do you want?" he asks.

John turns from the window, handling the transmitter with sweaty palms. "Do you remember me?" When Jameson shakes his head, John says in a reflective voice, "No, I guess you wouldn't." He sits back in his chair. "You were with the R.C.M.P. back then. I was hitchhiking with my mother."

At first the minister looks blankly at John, then his

face contorts and grows dark with memory.

"I was only fifteen then," John says, his face an image of stone. "You picked us up on the highway. You had a mustache and you had a big ring on your pinky finger." John sits forward and says coldly, "If you're smart enough to be scared to death, now's the time."

Sweat the colour of blood seeps from Jameson's pores. He reaches into his desk and pulls out a .38 snub-nose, a retired sidearm of the R.C.M.P..

"Go ahead," John says. "We'll both go out with a bang, and so will anyone else who hasn't cleared the building yet."

With the gun aimed at John's head, Jameson hesitates, then drops the weapon in defeat.

* * *

Outside the Indian Affairs building, Janet watches more protestors swelling the mass of the crowd. This new group comes from the mirrored building, secretaries in high heels, civil servants pulling on their coats, office boys joking together. The building is being evacuated, she thinks, and not just the Indian Affairs staff, the entire building, bank employees, janitors, travel consultants. When a short, frumpy woman pauses beside her on the sidewalk, Janet asks, "What's going on?"

"A gas leak. Everyone out." The woman stands on her toes, peering over heads, then waves one arm at someone in the crowd and plunges into the mass.

Janet turns, several R.C.M.P. and city police cars

pull up to the corner, including a special tactics team and what looks like a bomb squad. Also among the convoy are two paddy wagons. A man with a bullhorn, who has led the crowd chanting, "We will not let Jameson rule our lives," now urges them to be calm. Janet spots several plainclothes officers, including a couple who look to be in charge. She bolts their way. When she comes to the edge of the crowd near the police, she shouts, "What's happening here?" A number of other reporters have gathered with her at the curb. "And don't tell us this is only a precautionary measure."

When the reporters press closer, a sharply-dressed man steps forward. "We have a situation inside the building," he says. He looks down on the gathered reporters. "There's nothing more I can say at this point."

"A situation involving ARM?" Janet asks.

She can tell she's right by the way the man's eyes freeze on hers momentarily. But he says calmly, "We have a crisis on our hands. Let us deal with it. When we're ready, we'll make a statement. In the meantime, move away from the building." The officer turns and approaches the man with the bullhorn. They exchange words, then the Native leader addresses the crowd.

"They want us to stop the demonstration and move away from the building," he yells. Shouts of anger rise from the crowd. The man with the bullhorn has moved away from the police. He holds the instrument to his mouth.

"I say we cross the street and continue our peaceful

protest." The crowd shouts in agreement. Several cops run into the street and block traffic as the crowd migrates across Portage Avenue. Reporters armed with tape recorders and video cameras mill around, shooting the crowd, following the man with the bullhorn. Among them is Keith Morasty, some time cinematographer, sometime news camera man. He pushes up to Janet and says, "We got a tip that the last member of ARM is in the building. Someone said they saw him near the back entrance."

"Yes," Janet says. "He called in anonymously when the story broke."

"Holy shit, this is big," Keith says, rubbing his chin with the betacam resting on his shoulder. "I'm not sure the reporter we brought knows how to cover something like this. Where's Wayne?"

"Fuck if I know," she replies.

A plain-clothes cop approaches Janet through the crowd. When he catches her eye he asks, "Janet Fontaine?" Janet is startled. A lump has formed in her throat. "Could you come with me please. Now."

She turns to Keith. "Keep an eye on this. Until Wayne shows up or until I return, you're in charge here."

"But what can I do?"

"Improvise. Use your own people," Janet says. She nods at the cop. He takes her behind a police cordon toward a group of men beside an unmarked cruiser. One of the men steps forward and joins them as they make toward the south side of the Kensington Building. Looking up, Janet sees that the windows are cool and bright, nothing seems different. She wonders if she should object, but knows there's no point. She bites her lip and follows. They enter a van parked across the street from the Kensington Building. Inside are two more men, a Clint Eastwood type with a .44 magnum across his lap, and a tall Native man. They are dressed like combat troops, but their eyes are shifty, like cops'. Janet says, "This is getting heavy." She looks back over her shoulder. Across the street, the crowd is moving in a slow circle.

"You bet it is," the cop behind her says. He instructs her to sit down and when she takes the seat opposite the Native fellow, she sees he is quite young. The cop is saying, "The minister of Indian Affairs is being held hostage by a man identifying himself as the fourth member of ARM. He's wired with explosives which will be detonated by a radio transmitter if he is knocked down, shot, or harassed. We're trying to find the transmitter's frequency so we can jam its signal, but it takes time. We also know his identity and background. We're confident he can be reasoned with, but we need help."

"Me?" Janet asks. "I'm this help?"

"Not you. His brother. We need you to help us find Wayne Weenusk."

* * *

The kids are at school, Theresa is at work, the answering machine is on, and the front door is locked. Wayne sits in a corner of his basement holding a picture of his mother taken shortly before her death. In his other hand is a letter she wrote him from Kenora. Beside him is a solitary ashtray, which he's fashioned out of tin foil, filled with butts. His eyes are glazed. In them he sees an image of his mother. She's kneading dough to make bannock. Her hair is long, it hangs down to the middle of her back and catches light when she turns toward the windows. Like Theresa, she tucks a strand behind her ear as she works. Wayne's mother is singing softly, a song she learned from her mother, a song she taught Wayne. It started, 'I remember the neighbors talking, when my mother started night walking, that's what a rich man calls the spoils of war.' Wayne takes a drag from the cigarette. His mother. He thought she'd simply run off, as the authorities said she'd done. But all the while he'd hoped that either the rumors that she was killed were true, or that one day she'd return. These hopes and dreams became buried, but they never really disappeared.

Wayne thinks of a day when he came home late from work and Jason was asleep on the couch in the living room. He refused to go to his own bed, Theresa said, until he came home. The little boy's eyes were filled with tears. He thought his father was never coming home. Wayne places the letter on the floor beside the trunk in which he's left it for more than twenty years, and walks up the stairs to the kitchen. He stops at the living room. The hammering on the front door is relentless.

"Wayne, it's Janet," a voice he hardly recognizes says through the door. "I know you're in there. Open up, we have to talk."

Wayne sits on the couch. His eyes are far away, and the sounds he hears are those of his mother singing.

"Wayne, I talked to Theresa, she told me you were home. It's no use pretending."

Wayne stares at the door. Leave me alone, he thinks.

There is a massive thump, then another, and the door flies open. Wayne turns his eyes slowly and sees two men climbing off the floor. Beneath them is his front door.

"That door," he says, "cost two hundred bucks." His voice sounds far away, like it's coming from inside a wad of cotton.

"Wayne," Janet says. "It's about John." She stands in front of the two men, looking Wayne directly in the eye. "He's holding Jameson hostage at Indian Affairs and he's loaded with explosives. They want your help."

"You mean they want me to talk him into surrendering?" Wayne asks, standing up.

"By supplying us with information," one of the men says. He's Native, a young man wearing a flack jacket and army issue boots. "If it comes to surrender, that too."

Janet asks, "When did you last see him?"

Wayne turns and stares out the window. A slushy March stares back. The sky is blue and bright. The sun is getting higher, out of sight now above the window making shadows crisp and bold. "He was here all right, I didn't know that until this morning. He left before dawn. The bomb he has on him was made in the basement. You can check it out if you want."

"Maybe later," the Native man says. "Right now we'd like you to come downtown."

Wayne nods. "Don't you want to know what kind of device he has?"

The Native agent motions the others to leave the room. Once they're gone, he says, "Sit tight for a moment and hear me out. My name is Frank Lucas. I know your brother, man, I worked with him. I helped him blow up three buildings, and I bought the parts for the device he made in your basement. I was also working for CSIS, a plant."

Wayne shakes his head and says, "It doesn't wash. Why weren't they all arrested a long time ago? Two people would still be alive."

"We had to find the people really in charge. Your brother was only following orders. We finally did learn who was behind the operation, but they must have suspected because last night the R.C.M.P. walked in on us with guns blazing. I didn't know they were coming and I nearly got killed, too. Your brother got away. He went to dump excess explosives. I thought it was just luck, but today it looks like he may have known that the R.C.M.P. got tipped and who did it."

"Why do you say that?"

"Because he's holding Jameson hostage, and Jameson is in charge of ARM. We've picked up a woman who was also a member and she's agreed to talk. We have all the evidence we need to fry Jameson." Frank purses his lips together, letting this information sink in. Then he adds, "But we need him alive. That's where you come in. If you could get John to back down, then we'll be able to nail Jameson publicly. If he dies today, it might just make him a martyr. Do you under stand what I'm saying?"

Wayne looks into Frank's eyes and sees Native brotherhood. He nods.

* * *

On the corner of Portage and Smith the throng of four thousand is milling about chaotically. The protest has died, but everyone is still attentive. From time to time there is a rustle in the crowd and everyone looks up at the plate glass windows. But after a few moments the anticipation wanes. Dozens of uniformed police hold the crowd beyond the yellow cordon set up fifty feet from the building. Everyone knows about the bomb. The press huddle a few feet closer to the building, among them Keith with his betacam aimed at Jack, the weary NCN television news reporter. A frantic Walter Cook, reeling from the news of Elsie Moore's arrest, stands close by scrutinizing every word Jack utters. Above the street, lining building windows across from the Indian Affairs offices, R.C.M.P. and city police snipers battle the shiny mirrored windows trying to get John in their sights. In a van below, officers work with electronic equipment, trying to pinpoint the frequency of John's transmitter, but so far, nothing has registered except the telex and dozens of computers. They work patiently, fearful they might accidentally detonate the bomb themselves. The van carrying Wayne, Janet, and Frank drives through police lines and stops in front of the building. Frank and Wayne are immediately escorted into the building. Janet turns and makes her way through the crowd.

A dozen other reporters crowd in. "Wasn't that Wayne Weenusk," someone calls out. Janet smiles but keeps moving, enjoying the power of being in control.

Inside, Wayne and Frank take the elevator to the seventeenth floor. A special tactics officer nods toward the door where John is and then moves aside. Frank enters first, then motions Wayne to follow. "He's in the far office," Frank whispers. "Stay close and follow my lead." They move closer to the closed door, then duck behind a cubicle thirty feet away. Frank takes a breath as another agent, the Clint Eastwood type, joins them. Frank nods and the Clint Eastwood type stands up.

"John, are you there?" he yells.

"I'm here and so is the Minister. But unless you leave, we'll be all over the place."

Clint Eastwood ducks back down as Frank turns to Wayne. "Okay, this is where you come in. Acknowledge yourself, then walk over and enter the office, got it?"

"Got it," Wayne says. He stands up. "John, it's me." When there is no response from the office, Wayne says, "Wayne." Frank motions to keep walking, and Wayne swallows into a parched throat, but calmly steps forward. Looking out the windows, he can see the snipers lining the windows across the street, their high-powered rifles glinting in the sun. Wayne touches his brow. He's sweating. When he reaches the door he pushes it open slowly and repeats, "It's me, Wayne."

Inside, he finds John holding a gun, but sitting casually in an office chair and perspiring heavily. His cheeks are flushed and dark, tired circles rim his intense eyes. Behind the desk sits Cyrus Jameson. "So this is the guy," Wayne comments, closing the door behind him.

John motions for Wayne to be silent, then stands up and searches his brother's body. His hands, moving quickly over Wayne's torso, feel professional as a killer's, like the cops who frisked him downstairs. Again Wayne looks at Jameson. His contempt is too great for him to speak. But he feels the bile rising from his stomach to the back of his mouth.

"So," John says. "You here to get me to surrender?"

"Not really," Wayne says.

John looks puzzled. "Then what?"

Wayne looks from Jameson to his brother. "You lied to me," he says. "You told me mom ran out on us. You told me that she ditched you at Anishnabe Park."

"I was protecting you."

"You were playing God." Wayne looks around. "As usual."

"Listen you ungrateful shit. If I had told you the truth it might be you sitting here loaded with dynamite and in the sights of a hundred rifles. I knew the truth, and I knew mom's death had to be avenged. I saved you from the mission."

"Now you're the martyr as well as the hero."

"If that's what you think," John says, "go back to your television camera. Let me handle this alone."

Wayne looks out the window. Across on Smith Street he can see the NCN crew huddled around Janet. The CBC crew is closer to the building, near where the electronics van is parked. The man with the bullhorn is talking to police along the yellow cordon. Wayne turns and looks at John. His brother's face is glistening with sweat and the pockets beneath his eyes seem to have sunk deeper. John wipes at the sweat with his cuff, then touches his hair the way Wayne remembers their mother touched hers automatically when she was doing little household tasks.

Wayne sits down and says, "You've been alone for too long man, let me help out."

John snorts. "We're a bit short on options."

"Why don't we walk out of here?"

"Is this the surrender line?"

"No," Wayne says. "It's the sensible line." He walks closer to the window. "Besides, I love you, man, you're family."

"Spending the rest of my days in prison doesn't sound like too much of a life."

"And going out like this?" Wayne nods out the window.

Across the street in the Somerset building, a cop has John lined up for a clean shot. Two more are off to the left. Wayne looks down at the electronics van. On its roof is a directional finder, twitching in the cold, March air, looking for the clue that will jam John into oblivion. Wayne swallows the lump in his throat.

"How would it be if you knew this shit was rotting in prison as well?" he asks.

"He won't get convicted for mom's death. I was the only witness and my word is shit."

"But he's the guy behind your bombings, the silent boss. They've got all the evidence they need to convict him, no shit."

John turns and stares at Jameson. Then a wry smile fills his face. He laughs hard and with satisfaction. "So," he says, "I've been had again. The joke's on me after all." His face is alight with knowledge, first of his own gullibility, then of something new.

A bullet pierces the window directly behind John and hits him squarely between the shoulder blades, then a second and a third. The force of the bullets sends him twisting backward and he slams into the desk, spraying blood across the room. Wayne's shoes are covered, as is Jameson's neck. They look at each other. Wayne sees that Jameson's lips are trembling and he wipes his brow. Both of them stare at John, at the red casings of dynamite visible in John's parka.

Moments pass. Wayne hears the heavy breathing of Jameson and the restless noise from the crowd buzzing below. When it's clear the bomb will not go off, Jameson steps tentatively toward the door. Wayne turns his gaze to him. Then he looks at John's gun and picks it up. He imagines holding it directly between the Minister's eyes, the sharp report of one shot, Jameson's blood spurting out the back of his head and onto the wall. At the door Frank is saying,

"Careful, Wayne. He's no good to us dead."

"Maybe not," says Wayne, through gritted teeth, "but..."

"But nothing. I know about your mother, but this is not vengeance we're after here, it's justice. Remember?" He's silent and then adds after several moments, "Don't waste what your brother did for you. For all of us."

Wayne stares into Jameson's eyes searching for the killer and the rapist, searching for defiance, searching for whatever it is that drives a man to murder, but all he finds are frightened eyes. Nothing worth shooting.

"All right," he says.

"All right," Frank agrees.

* * *

Downstairs, Wayne steps into a March morning. The sky is bright and the dark clouds on the horizon earlier have broken up. He looks about, scanning the protestors and curiosity seekers. Thousands of eyes stare back, but Wayne casually walks to the press line where Janet is standing by with the NCN television news crew.

"Are you all right?" Janet asks. Wayne nods and takes the mike from her.

"Ready?" he asks Keith.

"Rolling."

Wayne raises the mike: "The Minister of Indian and Northern Affairs sits in his office facing criminal charges while the fourth member of the terrorist group, ARM, lies dead." He lowers the mike for a moment and looks into the sky to collect his thoughts. All about him it is silent.

"John Weenusk was killed today by an R.C.M.P. rifle. He had masterminded the bombings of the St. Jean's Basilica in Montreal, the Labatt's Brewery in Toronto, and the Hudson's Bay department store in Winnipeg. John came here to face Cyrus Jameson, the Minister of Indian and Northern Affairs who, as it became clear today, was the real power behind ARM. John Weenusk was a terrorist. He fought for what he believed in. Ironically, he was a pawn of what he fought against. The real function of ARM was to turn public sympathy against Native people. It would have created an opportune time for Jameson to push his new, controversial bill through the House of Commons, and undo what Native people have struggled to attain for over two hundred years. Jameson failed. Perhaps he felt threatened by the political and economic power that is developing among Native people.

"A hundred years ago we were the 'Native problem,' shuffled onto reserves in the hope that we would go away, but we didn't. We fought against oppression. We fought with knives and rifles, we fought with our hearts, we fought to get educated, and we fought in the courts. John Weenusk fought another battle and died in victory. Cyrus Jameson will go to prison. Native people have won their chance to be their own masters again."

EXPOSURE

"Turbulence," the flight attendant explained, "the sky over Saskatchewan is full of turbulence. Fasten your seat belt, keep the white bag close at hand, and enjoy the rest of the flight. Lunch will be along shortly."

"Lunch?" Kris Morris asked, "with all this turbulence?"

"Don't matter none if the ride's bumpy, the food still sucks," replied a twelve year old in the window seat. The kid poked his glasses further up his nose and continued. "Don't worry mister, if you've flown in planes as much as me, you'd get used to this bumpy stuff." Kris smiled politely, hoping the kid would shut his face. The plane lurched as more turbulence hit.

"Whoa!" the kid wailed.

Kris could feel his stomach trying to bail out. His hand prepared to grab the white bag, but the plane corrected itself. A collective groan passed through economy. An elderly lady a few rows back noisily passed wind.

"You don't fly much, do you mister?" the kid asked.

"More than I'd like to."

"Where you headed?"

"Bonedry."

"Bonedry," the kid responded with a contorted

expression. "Where the fuck is that?"

Where the fuck indeed, Kris thought. A no-count town in the middle of nowhere is how an outsider might describe it. It had a grain elevator, all Saskatchewan towns do. Was it home? Not really, but it was the closest town near home. The only town near home. A mere mile from the reserve, but a long way from Toronto. He hadn't been back in fifteen years. Not since he'd gone back to see his old flame, Bev Pratt. She had a miscarriage that summer. Fifteen years, Kris thought to himself, then turned to look out the window. Billowy fluffs of white hung suspended from the blue sky above. The land seemed surreal from high altitude. A vast, miniature display not unlike toy store windows, but somehow infinite. Within the walls of minute houses in minute towns scattered across the parched land, there were miniature people living miniature lives. In a house down there could be a family. Were they happy, were they poor, was it a farm on the brink of foreclosure? Their struggles, were they real, or fabricated merely for the sake of display? Was the family aware they were on display, that thirty thousand feet above, a plane hummed and eighty people passed by sipping soft drinks and munching stale peanuts, each with their own struggles, real or fabricated.

The twelve year old's face still displayed curiosity, wondering if the big Indian beside him had gone deaf. "Why you going back?" he asked.

Kris watched another town slip towards the horizon. What if it were a town like Bonedry, near a reserve like his, with a family like his? Then it wouldn't be a fabrication, it wouldn't be a display, it would be real.

"I'm gonna help out my brother, he's moving."

The twelve year old looked away, his interest in the big Native waning. The plane entered a new stage of lurch. It dropped a few hundred feet and bumped and swayed about. The elderly lady a few rows back passed another gush of wind.

"Whoa!" the kid wailed.

Kris gripped his seat and gritted his teeth. "These be turbulent times," he chimed.

*　*　*

Kris had two brothers, Martin, two years younger, and Ralph, three years older. When they were young they had lived on a reserve, and like all other children on reserves, were taken away from home and sent to boarding school. Ralph was the first to go. He was bullied by older boys, had his hair chopped off, and the Cree language beaten out of him. He came back that first summer and told his younger brothers what it was like, then begged his parents not to send him back. The parents lamented, but sent him back anyway. Ralph died of typhoid. On his deathbed, he begged his parents not to let his younger brothers be taken to the boarding school.

"They take away your dignity and then you die," Ralph told them.

The parents grieved for their eldest child, and promised Kris and Martin they would never go to the wicked place where their brother had died. They grieved long and hard, then their father found that booze helped dull the pain.

The drinking created havoc within the family, and at times, Kris wondered if he and Martin wouldn't be better off in the boarding school. The booze made their father crazy and he would beat their mother. Martin would huddle in his bed and cry. Kris would hold his little brother and rock him gently back and forth while whispering stories in the young boy's ear. Martin would fall asleep, then Kris would cry. Sometimes, when the beatings lasted a long time, he wished his father would die.

It happened one spring. In a drunken stupor, their father grabbed his whiskey and walked onto a frozen slough a mile from home. The ice broke and their father sunk to his waist. He leaned over, placing his upper body on the ice, and rested. He was found three days later. "Exposure," the doctor wrote, "death by exposure."

Kris felt guilt for wishing his father dead, but from then on, when he and Martin would venture outdoors, not an inch of their skin would be open to the wind and air, in case they too fell victim to exposure.

Their mother, mourning another death, buckled under the grief. "Breakdown," the doctor said, "she had a nervous breakdown."

Kris put Martin on his knee that day.

"Remember when I said I could only tell the snake story when we needed it?" Martin's little head nodded, aware of his brother's serious tone. Kris told him what had happened, then told the story as Martin cried. "There was a snake," Kris began, "a green snake who lived in a slough..."

Kris and Martin were taken in by Aunt Peggy Jane, who already had five kids of her own. She tried to support every one, but it was hard. Food and clothing were difficult to obtain. When September came, Kris and Martin were sent to the boarding school. They both vividly remembered Ralph's description of what boarding school was like, and when they arrived, all that Ralph had told them turned out to be true. It was a sad, desolate place. When they first walked in the door, Martin told Kris he was scared. A nun, overhearing them, whipped Martin across the face with a stick for speaking Cree. At night, Martin would cry. Kris would leave his bunk and march past all the other crying children to hold his little brother. As Martin whimpered, Kris rocked him back and forth and whispered stories into his little brother's ear. Not loud enough for the nuns to hear, but loud enough so Martin could hear him over the other crying children.

There was always crying at night, among the younger ones especially, huddled alone in the dark, crying for moms, for the warmth of kookum, to be anywhere else but this ugly building where a supreme god didn't want them to speak Cree or remain Indian, and so hired a priest and a pack of nuns to frighten, oppress, and defeat them. They were children in prison, in concentration camps where the church strived to alter their minds and their lives forever.

"See you mister," said the kid by the window. Kris waved goodbye and walked down the aisle to the exit. A flight attendant thanked him and wished him well, and Kris mumbled thanks and stepped off the plane. The dry prairie air sucked moisture from his lips and throat as he squinted from the midday sun bouncing off the tarmac. It was miserably hot. Beads of sweat formed on his nose and forehead before he reached the terminal, and the word stuck in his mind. Terminal, mortal, death.

The building was air conditioner cool. Kris waited for his luggage and watched for his brother, expecting an emaciated, sickly fragment of a body.

* * *

The news had been a shock. Kris was busy working when Martin's call came through. Martin had told the secretary it was important and the secretary had passed the call through. Kris excused himself from a meeting and took the call in his office. He knew it was a crisis. Why else would Martin call?

"What's up?" Kris asked.

And Martin told him, "I'm sick." Kris left the meeting, the company lost the sale, and he nearly lost his job. He told his boss, "I'm sorry, but my brother is dying. I need some time off." Kris asked for a month. He got two weeks.

"I have to go to Regina," Kris told Karina, his roommate and lover. "Martin's sick, he wants to move

162

back to the reserve and die there."

"Are you all right?"

"I'll get through it," he said tersely, thinking back to boarding school. In troubled times, he always thought back to boarding school. If I made it through that, he rationalized, I can make it through anything. He stood at the living room window staring at an indifferent city. Skyscrapers filled the sky, cars buzzed beneath webs of wires, and hookers patrolled the street below. A faint quiver came to his lips as his eyes glazed over. The city became a distant light at a tunnel's end as his thoughts turned to his mother.

"The Creator tests us to keep us strong," she once told him. "Your father's drinking is a test. When we are through it, we will be stronger."

He thought back to his recent telephone conversation with Martin.

"Have you told mom?" Kris had asked.

"I'm afraid to," Martin replied. "It might cause a relapse."

"I suppose," Kris said, drumming a swizzle stick against the phone. "It's giving me a relapse."

"What's he dying of?" Kris' head jerked, snapping him from thought. He turned away from the city and stared at Karina. She was a beautiful woman with dark hair and blue eyes. A colour combination that fascinated Kris. Her petite frame and fair skin had also attracted him. Her blue eyes stared into his, seeking, perhaps prying, but the frown in her eyebrows reflected concern. "What's he dying of?" she repeated.

The glaze over Kris' eyes turned to ice. He walked

past her to the bedroom and started packing.

* * *

The airport was nearly empty. Kris sat in the waiting area leaning across his soft luggage. Martin was late, but this allowed Kris time to relax. He shut his eyes, trying to picture the reserve. Would the rolling hills still seem like hills? Would the road still be shit? Would the old house still be standing?

"Hey!" a voice said, "you can't crash here, this is a public place. Who do you think you are, Indian?"

Kris opened his eyes, squinting against the light. "Eh, Martin?" Kris sat up and examined his brother. "You're looking good," he said, lying. Martin's body was thin, strikingly thin, and it showed in his face. Only his eyes, deep brown and alert, seemed healthy.

Martin smiled, then grabbed a piece of luggage. "I've got a car outside."

Kris stood, suddenly aware of his advancing age. Was it more energy he had in his twenties, or an inability to relax? They walked out to the parking lot. The car was a wreck. A windshield-cracked, muffler-punctured, rusted out wreck. Kris sat amidst ripped upholstery and searched for his seat belt.

"Don't bother," Martin advised, "there aren't any."

The heat was asphyxiating. Martin's fingers danced across the hot, manual steering wheel as he veered the car noisily from the airport. A trail of smoke billowed in their wake. Kris sat sweating, wondering if he would survive the drive, or would the double greenhouse effect shrivel him prune-like. At least the electric windows worked. Kris watched Martin press the buttons, then heard the reluctant whir as the glass panes rose from within the rust ridden, green doors. He had a mind to protest, but thought Martin's need for heat might be because of his disease. For his brother's comfort, he grinned and sweated. Then came a miracle. Martin reached down and pressed a few more buttons. Amidst a cloud of dust, cool air filtered through the vents. Kris absorbed the cold with the lust of a voracious pig. He wallowed in it and opened his shirt to feel its touch against his clammy skin.

"How's that for luxury," Martin chimed, and then added apologetically, "It gobbles a lot of gas."

They drove past the city of Regina, content in their fridge-like comfort, then stopped on the outskirts to fill up; a thirty dollar fill up. They also stopped to fill up in Lestock.

"Maybe there's a leak in the gas tank," Martin suggested. When Kris didn't respond, he added, "Maybe it's a shitty car. A reserve car."

Then came Bonedry, the name written in bold, blue letters upon the ragged, grain elevator. They left the highway and crossed the tracks.

"Two more miles 'til we hit the rez," Martin said.

"I thought it was one," Kris countered.

It was only one. The road turned from provincial asphalt to reserve gravel; mud when it was wet. The houses they passed were distinctively reserve, cheap paint-covered, porchless square boxes without fancy trimmings. Often clustered together in three or four depending on the size of the family. They passed the Pow Wow grounds, the band office, and the school, then pulled onto a dirt road just beyond the Anglican church established by Charles Cowley Pratt. Bev Pratt was a part of that family. Her house, Kris noted, was a mile away. Would she still be there? They pulled off the main road onto a weed covered driveway that led to an empty looking shack. Martin stopped the car and the brothers got out, staring silently at the place where their earliest memories lay.

The prairie was silent, save for the wind and shimmering leaves. Flies and butterflies flew about the shack collapsing slowly in the shade of poplar trees and advancing bush. An impression, Kris thought, that's all it is. The windows were gone and weeds had forced their way through the floor inside the front door. The door itself lay out front, cracked and splintered. Exposure, Kris said to himself. The wood was grey, having suffered from years of exposure to the harsh, prairie elements. It used to be turquoise. He could remember when his father painted it. Their mother had brooded for days over what the colour should be. They bought the paint in Bonedry, and the three of them, Dad, Kris, and Ralph transformed the wood shell into a colorful home. There was a sidewalk, windows, and almost a lawn. In this place, his earliest memories formed. He wondered at the years which separated that home from the grey, cracked structure which stood before him, suffocating under the encroaching bush. It was a memorial to an earlier time, and now only an impression of its former self.

"It looks different," Martin observed, leaning against the car door, "but it's still standing."

Kris walked up and stood beside his brother, still contemplating the shack. It was still standing, he agreed. They still had something to work with. Something to salvage.

* * *

"It's about time you two came back," their aunt wailed. "You still got family here, people remember you."

Some things never change, Kris thought. Sure, their aunt's house was different. There was a washer and dryer now, a microwave, a carpet. A successful merger of technology and the old home. Quite unlike the shack they'd return to during breaks from school. Their cousins had done well. Two were on the band council and they had rewarded their mother with modern appliances for her years of child-rearing. Yet the house had the same feel. Both men felt this as they took everything in. Familiarity came slowly, but surely. Their aunt spoke with the same authoritative tone. The scowl, though buried under more wrinkles, was essentially the same. The grin still toothless.

"I got new teeth," she said proudly. "Tommy bought 'em in Regina. I put them in when I go out or if there's company." Her gums smacked noisily. "But you two ain't company, so I don't put 'em in. How long you gonna stay?" She spoke with a strong Cree accent.

Martin and Kris looked at each other.

"It depend,." Kris said.

"On what?" she pressed.

Kris again looked at Martin. Martin nodded.

"On how long Martin lives."

The aunt stared at the younger brother. She shook her head and lowered it, then took a deep breath and looked across the table and out the window. The pain of three generations was clearly etched in the corners of her sad eyes.

Martin cleared his throat. "I've come back, Auntie, because I want to die on the reserve. I'm going to move back to my parents' house."

"You want to live in that old shack?"

"Kris will help me fix it up."

Aunt Peggy Jane turned to look at Kris. "This is what people choose for death when they get a choice?"

Kris shrugged.

"The place is still in your names, so the band'll fix it up for you if you want," she said, wiping the glaze from her eyes. "You'll find lots of changes here. The reserve ain't like it used to be."

* * *

Martin sat in his motel room staring at the half-full moon. It was a still night except for the wind, which blew dust and bits of debris past Martin's window. Any stronger, Martin thought, and it would blow away the moon. He sucked on the nail of his index finger as he stared, his eyes like a scared child's, his breath heavy and short. He glanced down to the fields of grain lit softly by the moon, and then to his feet. With the nail clippers loaded, he reached down to clip his toenails, grey and neglected, then stopped half way, his face wincing in pain. Slowly he sat up, his teeth grinding against the hurt. When the pain had subsided, he reached to the nightstand and grabbed a bottle of pills. He threw painkillers into his mouth, then grabbed another bottle and downed several antibiotics -- septra, norfloxicin. There were three more bottles of pills he turned to before drinking a glass of water. He sat back, breathing deeply until the suffering passed, then reached down to his toenails again. This time, he made it, but he could feel the tumors despite the pills. Inside him, they were growing, unwanted invaders spreading through his body. He sat up and again stared through the window with the nail clippers twiddling between his fingers. His eyes glazed over and he lay down, his body limp.

* * *

In the bar, Kris sat with Frank Morris who was Aunt Peggy Jane's youngest son and a member of the reserve's band council. With a belly the size of a bread box, Frank was a comical contrast to his more fit cousin. Sharing a pitcher of beer and watching golf highlights on the big screen in the corner, the cousins chatted.

"You don't see many good looking girls in this bar," Frank complained. He cleared his throat and added, "Must be some hot looking babes in Toronto, huh?"

"A few," Kris admitted, his eyes were wandering the bar. "Aren't you married?" he asked.

"Yeah, yeah," Frank mumbled.

Kris watched Ben Crenshaw sink a thirty foot putt, then turned to his younger cousin and said, "Martin and I are moving into our parents' old house." His voice was serious. "Can we get the band to fix it up?"

Frank took a breath, then a swig of his beer. "There's a waiting list longer than my dick," he said. "Everyone and his dog has put in requests for housing. The construction boys are busier than shit." He paused as a woman across the bar caught his eye. "Wow! Check her out, she gets better looking every year."

Kris turned and looked in the direction that Frank's lips pointed. Across the room, beneath the golf highlights, Bev Pratt sat down. Kris' glance lingered, his eyes stuck on her. Bev's hair was long, perhaps to her waist. She was in her early thirties, but could pass for twenty-seven. If she had kids, you couldn't tell by her figure. She was beautiful, just as beautiful as Kris remembered.

"Your best bet," Frank continued, jarring Kris back to earth, "is to put in a claim for repairs, but go ahead and do them yourself. I'll make sure you're reimbursed for the costs. This way it gets done and you come out even. Otherwise, you could be waiting for months, even years."

"Could you put me at the top of the list?"

"Two years ago maybe, but not anymore. Shit would hit the fan and I don't like shit."

"Fair enough," Kris said. "Have any tools I can borrow?"

Frank laughed as Kris turned back to the big screen, now showing football highlights. His eyes shifted to Bev, hoping to sneak in a stare, but she was looking right at him. For a moment, they stared at each other, dumfounded expressions plastered on their faces. Then suddenly, Bev stood up and walked out.

Frank laughed. "Ha! You spooked her," he said.

Kris grabbed a beer and took a large gulp, hoping to wash his stomach out of his throat.

* * *

It was like clearing cobwebs. Backtracking through his brain seeking images, seeking memories. Kris' face contorted, trying to visualize the past. He remembered their first time together, his first time ever. In retrospect, it was his clumsiness that stood out, and her patience.

It was summer and they had been seeing each other since school ended. One night, they found themselves alone at her house. Her father was at the bar, her mother at bingo, and her brother and sister asleep. She must have seen the eagerness in his eyes.

She laid back and spread herself open for him. He climbed on top and watched her pain when he entered. He thrust and she bit her lip, he thrust again, and again, and it was over. He collapsed on top of her, feeling guilty and repulsed. He climbed off and laid beside her, avoiding her eyes. She wiped away the blood and semen with a dirty sheet. He dressed and walked home feeling different. He had done something wrong and the stars and the trees frowned on him. The next night, he returned, and again she accepted him. When it was over, he wasn't so repulsed. He went home that night with a smile on his face. But the smile disappeared when his aunt began sniffing as he entered the house. His guilt returned. Aunt Peggy Jane left the room, then came back with a box of condoms.

"Use them," she instructed. It took him and Bev a few minutes to figure out how, but they never went without again, except once.

The big screen was a blur, as was the rest of the world. Kris tried to focus, his head wavering, his lips hanging. Occasionally, spittle streamed out.

"You drunk?" Frank asked.

It took some seconds for Kris' reply. "I'm not drunk, just feeling good," he slurred. Drops of spit spread across the table. "Are you drunk?"

"Yup!" Frank blurted. "I'm scared to stand up cause I might fall."

With determination, Kris stood up. "Nothin' to it," he burbled, struggling to keep his balance. "Goodnight."

Like a wet rag, Kris swaggered through the bar. The walk out took him past a forest of faces, many he thought he recognized. His eyes shifted slowly, trying to catch sight of a door with a red exit above it. He found three and aimed for the closest one.

The night was hot. Not like a Toronto hot, but a Regina hot. A dry, searing hot. And the night was dark, unlike Toronto, too. Kris walked into a small field beside the motel so he could see the night. Wavering, he stared into the sky and saw a brilliant collage of stars. In drunken awe, he stared. The sky was dotted with more stars than he had seen in twenty years. The effect was dizzying and Kris' legs gave out. He looked down in time to see the ground come up and smack him in the face. Then he rolled over and stared at the stars again.

He remembered he used to look at the stars quite often while lying in a field. A few times while making love with Bev, but most when he was younger and would sneak out of his dorm at school at night. Like the night he followed the nuns when they took Martin away. It was the third time they did that. The previous times, Martin came back crying. Kris tried talking to him, but Martin wouldn't respond. He just lay there and cried until Kris held him in his arms and rocked him back and forth, telling him in whispers that they'd borrow guns from Eddie Thomas and shoot all the nuns.

When they took Martin away from the building, Kris followed. Briskly they crossed the short distance to the priest's house. Kris could hear his brother whimpering. The nuns knocked on the side door while Kris hid behind a hedge. The door was opened, then shut, and the nuns walked away. Quietly, Kris moved along the side of the house. He stood up and peered into the window, but saw only dim silhouettes. He tried another window. It was too dark, but under the door he could see slivers of light bouncing through. He turned around a corner of the house and headed for the window of what he guessed was the living room. The bright yellow light shone out, lighting a patch on the grass behind Kris as he slowly raised himself up. With his eyes wide open, he looked in. The priest was standing in the middle of the room, grinning, his pants around his ankles. Martin was bent over in front. Kris' face twisted in shock and repulsion before he quickly spun to the ground. Undetected, he moved through the night back to the main building, pausing once to vomit, and silently slipped back into his bed. When Martin was returned later that night, he was crying. For a while, Kris listened to his brother's cries, then drowned them out by pulling his blanket over his ears. As Martin's sobs continued, Kris fell asleep. He never held Martin in his arms again.

The wind was rattling the grass and the weeds. Kris stuck his head up and looked around. The motel was some seventy-five metres to his left. In the other direction, there was infinite black. Above were the stars, the moon, the wisps of northern lights. Kris stared at the motel, then at a nearby vendor where dozens were milling about. A line from the vendor extended into the parking lot. Car trunks were open and there was a fight by a ratty Ford pickup. Kris' head sunk back to the ground.

"What the fuck am I doing here?" he asked himself.

* * *

Martin gargled and spat. The mouthwash spewed through the open window, landed in the hot dust, and formed little balls of mud at Kris' feet.

"Watch it," Kris yelled.

"Sorry," Martin replied. He lathered his face with shaving gel and started to shave.

Kris turned his attention back to the house and scrutinized a week's worth of repairs. The windows had all been replaced once the frames were strengthened. They stood out next to the rest of the house, though, still weathered and beaten. Kris sighed at the amount of work yet to do, then turned to the front steps. He paused there to inspect his carpentry. Overall, he was satisfied, despite having run out of lumber to complete the last rung. Trying to shake the morning's lethargy, he bounced up and into the house. Martin was fixing a bowl of cereal.

"How are you feeling?" Kris asked, his standard question.

"Like shit," Martin replied, his stock answer.

Kris walked past the kitchen and into the bathroom, little more than a closet with a mirror and wash basin. He took a new bar of soap and a toothbrush out of a little duffle bag in the corner and washed up.

"I thought we'd check out the health clinic and let them know I'm here," Martin yelled from the kitchen.

"Good idea," Kris answered. He was lathering his face with shaving gel. He looked at his razor pensively, then extracted the blade and threw it in the garbage.

*　*　*

Kris had hated hospitals since his mother was taken away and left in one. The reserve's clinic was nowhere near as intimidating as a big hospital was, but Kris fidgeted anyway. Beside him in the waiting room were a mother and a baby. He wasn't familiar with babies, but this one couldn't have been more than a month old. And the mother couldn't have been more than sixteen.

"Mr. Morris?" Kris looked up and saw a young man dressed in white. The blue eyes and nervous attitude told Kris this boy was not from the reserve. "If you could step this way, I'd like to talk to you," the doctor said, motioning towards a small office. Kris rose and followed.

The walls were empty, unlike most doctor's offices Kris had seen in the past. He expected pictures of kids, degrees, things of that sort. "How long have you been working here?" Kris asked.

"I'm only here for the summer," the young, blue-eyed doctor answered. "I thought it would be a good learning experience to work on a reserve."

"Good for you," Kris replied half-heartedly.

"I've just spoken with your brother and I offered to talk to you concerning his condition. He thought it would be helpful," the doctor said. "As you know, your brother has AIDS. At this point there is no cure and the disease is terminal. Although your brother seems healthy right now, his immune system is very weak and he could get ill at any time. His health will only deteriorate, despite occasional periods when the infections are in remission. He's let us know about his condition so we can treat him safely and know what to expect. You should know what to expect, too."

Kris nodded.

"If you have any questions, call me and we'll talk."

Kris looked down at the wooden floor. "I have one," he said. "How can I protect myself?"

The doctor almost rolled his blue eyes, but sighed instead. "There's a lot of paranoia surrounding AIDS, but it's very difficult to contract. Day to day contact, such as sharing a glass of water, breathing the same air, or using the same comb, won't do it. Don't be afraid to hug either, 'cause in the next few months, your brother will need a lot of them." The young doctor paused, then leaned back in his chair and looked at Kris earnestly. "This won't be a picnic, understand that clearly."

Martin left the clinic in higher spirits. Kris left enlightened, but scared. The car roared from the parking lot, leaving dust to settle on the walls and window sills of the white building.

"How are you feeling?" Kris asked, dread in his voice.

"Like shit," Martin chirped.

They drove to the band office with the car protesting much of the way. Kris sorted receipts as Martin parked. Martin watched his brother total up seven bills.

"This is costing you a lot, isn't it?" Martin asked.

"Yup," Kris replied. "But I'll get it all back."

Kris shoved the receipts in his pocket before stepping into the hot sun. "You coming in?" he asked.

"I'll wait here," said Martin, still in a good mood.

Kris turned and walked into the band office. It was morning, so the building was close to empty. A secretary struggling with a computer was the only person Kris could see. He walked up to her and cleared his throat.

"Yeah?" she asked.

"Is Frank Morris here?"

She zapped a button on the telephone box. A moment later, Frank appeared from around a corner. "Kris," he said heartily. "You look healthier than the last time I saw you."

"So do you," Kris laughed, "I've got some receipts here."

"Right, I'll get the secretary to write a cheque. Can I see them?"

Kris pulled the wad from his pocket. "The total is in there somewhere."

"No problem," Frank assured, "I'll have the cheque for you in a second."

When Frank disappeared around the corner, Kris sat down and picked up a newspaper published by a Native press in Winnipeg. HUDSON'S BAY BOMBED BY ARM, the headline read. A tall man sat down beside Kris and when Kris looked up he noticed several moles on the man's neck.

"I'm James Caribou," the man said.

Kris nodded and shook the man's hand. "Kris Morris," he answered.

"Morris, any relation to Ernie Morris?" James asked.

"He's my uncle."

"So your Mitch Morris' son?"

Kris nodded. James looked away towards a map on the wall showing the province's reserves and Metis communities. "I knew your father," James said. "He was a friend."

"It happened a long time ago," Kris said.

"So it did. What brings you back to the reserve?"

"My brother and I are fixing up my dad's old house."

"Glad to hear it, but don't expect any help from the band. Our waiting list is already a mile long." Just then Frank reappeared and motioned Kris to follow him outside. The sky was still cloudless, the sun still hot, the wind still blew. Kris and Frank approached the car and Kris got in. After nodding once quickly to Martin, Frank reached into his pocket, pulled out a piece of paper, and handed it to Kris.

"There's your money," he said. "I didn't want to give it to you inside. James is a real stickler when it comes to things like this."

"Thanks," said Kris.

The brothers watched Frank march back into the band office. In a roar of dust and smoke, Martin started the car.

* * *

The last time Kris had seen his mother was on a trip to Winnipeg for a conference. She was healthy, but neurotic. The time before that was in Toronto, then in Brandon, and another half dozen times since he left the reserve. On each visit (and between) her mental health was always a concern. She had been improving each year, but for fear another emotional shock would set her back, Martin hadn't told her he was sick. Though Kris agreed with him, they both knew their mother had to know, and telling her would prove more difficult as time progressed. Their chance came when she showed up at Aunt Peggy Jane's.

Kris was working on the roof fixing a leak and at the same time avoiding Martin who was moving the stove into place in the kitchen.

"How are you feeling?" Kris asked again that morning.

"I'm feeling terrific," Martin said with exasperation. The doctor had warned Kris about times when Martin's moods would swing, so Kris took refuge on the roof.

The wind blew dust in his face, but Kris enjoyed the solitude and the height. He could see over the bush and down the dirt road until it curved toward the church. Wiping sweat from his face, he drew his hammer back several inches and hammered a nail through a shingle into the roof. It was time-consuming work, but mindless and therapeutic. Between hammer blows, Kris could hear Martin struggling with the stove below. The healthy, happy facade was wearing thin, and so was Martin's patience. His hair was dry and thin from the illness and matted with sweat as he tried to move the stove against the wall. Each time he pressed his body against the metal and heaved, his tumors squeezed a muffled cry of pain out of his mouth. The incessant hammering above added to his torment.

"Would you quit the fucking hammering," he yelled. The hammering stopped.

Kris leaned forward, a stream of sweat pouring into his eye, and looked through a small hole into the kitchen. Martin sat slumped against the stove, then slowly got to his knees. He stared at the stove, then rose up and walked out the back. Kris shook his head. Deciding it was time to rest, he leaned back on his elbows and stared into the sky. A small cloud, barely visible but the only one around, floated toward him. Kris' eye tracked it until it was straight above. There it seemingly disappeared, boiled away by the sun, and Kris felt the heat even more. Another cloud formed in the west, but this one was dust. A car was zooming down the road toward the house. Kris waited for it to turn away with the main road, but it slowed down and entered the long, bumpy driveway. Company, Kris thought, people, new faces to look at.

It was a late model Ford Bronco, but aging fast. By the time it pulled to a stop in front of the house, Kris was already off the roof and waiting by Martin's car. The Bronco door opened and Frank stepped out.

"Eh, Frank," Kris said, smiling.

Frank nodded, but didn't smile. "Your mother's here," he said.

The news gave Kris a jolt. He ran his fingers through his hair and let out a little sigh. "Where is she?"

"My mother's. I'm going to bring her here right away, but I thought I should warn you first."

"Does she know Martin's sick?"

"I don't know," Frank answered, stepping back into the Bronco. The door shut and Frank's head poked out the window. "I'll be back in about an hour."

Kris watched the dust rise in the Bronco's wake, then get swept away in the wind. A hot, dusty wind. Martin walked up to the front door. "Who was that?" he asked.

Kris kicked at a lump of weeds, then looked back as the Bronco wound out of sight. "It was Frank. Mom's at Aunt Peggy Jane's."

Martin turned and went back inside. He walked into the bathroom and filled up the wash basin. First, he dabbed some cream on a kleenex and removed layers of makeup before washing his face with soap. Next, he washed his thin, ratty hair, then towelled off and stared at himself in the mirror. With out the makeup and without the hat, the red patches on his face and scalp stood out clearly. In the corner of the mirror, Martin saw movement. He spun and found Kris standing in the doorway.

"What's all that?" Kris asked, his eyes focusing on the red patches on Martin's face.

"Kaposi's sarcoma," Martin replied. "Cancer."

"And you cover it with makeup?" Kris asked. Martin nodded. Kris turned and walked down the hall and Martin turned back to the mirror. He reached into the medicine cabinet and took out a makeup case and bottle, then smeared his face with a foundation.

Kris was on the front steps when Martin emerged and sat down beside him. Kris looked at his brother. "The makeup helps," he said. "You look a lot better."

"Thanks," Martin answered. "How are we going to tell mom?"

Before Kris could answer, the sound of a vehicle approached in the distance. Martin and Kris looked down the road as Frank's Ford Bronco came into sight. When the Bronco stopped behind Martin's green car, the passenger door opened and Ruby Morris stepped out. The brothers both smiled hard as their mother walked forward. Her stride was slow, but smooth, her face weathered, but healthy, her eyes sad, but alert. Kris noticed her left eye, always a bit lower than her right, had fallen a bit more. It looked more like a St. Bernard's eye than a human's. It always had.

She walked directly to Martin and looked him over, once down and once up, then she put her hands to her mouth. "You're so thin," she managed. Martin nodded. Kris watched his mother closely, thinking back to when his father died and how her face went blank. It stayed that way for a long time. "What are you sick with?" she asked.

When Martin didn't respond, Kris said, "Maybe we should go inside." He turned to Frank. "Could you wait out here for a while?"

Frank nodded, probably happy to stay outside. Kris and Martin turned to enter the house, but Ruby stood still. For the first time, she looked at the home she and her husband had moved into more than thirty years earlier. With her hands again over her mouth, she stepped forward, careful not to trip on the stairs. Martin and Kris looked at each other, but didn't speak. When their mother entered the room, she eased herself into a chair and sighed aloud as she settled back, resting her cane across her knees. She took a cloth from her purse, removed her glasses, then wiped her face. She was tired, Kris thought, and he was worried. She stared at the floor for several seconds, then looked up into Martin's eyes.

"Why didn't you tell me before?" she asked.

Martin turned away from her and looked out the window into the backyard where dragon flies ate smaller bugs. Would science come up with something to destroy the bug that was destroying him? "I was afraid to," he told her, still staring out the window. "I was afraid it would be too much for you."

"Look at me when you talk," she commanded. Martin breathed deep and obeyed. Moisture built up in both their eyes.

"You thought it better I'd find out after you died, without a chance to say goodbye?" she asked, her voice heavy with hurt. Martin wanted to look away, but he couldn't. Her eyes searched through him, penetrating the walls. "All right," she said. "What are you sick with?" Martin turned to Kris and motioned with his eyes towards the door. Kris left the room and the house. He marched down the stairs, almost tripped, and came to a halt under the sun. He breathed deeply for a few seconds trying to shake off the grief. Frank stepped out of the Bronco and walked over to his cousin. He looked the house over and nodded approval.

"The place looks a hundred percent better, no doubt about it," he said. "Keep turning in the receipts. This must be costing you a bundle."

"The repairs are only the half of it."

"Martin?"

"He has such swings in mood. One moment he's up and happy, the next as black as night."

Suddenly Ruby emerged from the house and walked straight to the Bronco. "Frank," she yelled. "Take me back to your mother's." Frank hesitated for a moment, his forehead wrinkled in confusion, then he stepped into the car. When the motor started, Ruby leaned out her window. "Kris," she called. Kris had been staring at her, his own forehead wrinkled. "I'm gonna stay at Aunt Peggy Jane's. She has more room over there." With a rattle, the vehicle drove away. Kris watched it disappear, suddenly understanding his mother's strange behaviour. He turned and walked back into the house, being careful as he went up the stairs. When he entered the kitchen, he found Martin staring out the window. Kris sat down.

"So what happened?" he asked.

"She didn't go crazy, she just left." Martin shrugged and turned to Kris. "She didn't say a word."

"It's a shock to her," Kris reasoned, tracing the wood pattern on the table with his fingernail. "Give her a few days and she'll come around."

"It's like she's more hurt that I'm gay than she is of me dying."

Kris chewed on the skin over his thumb, then dropped his hand to the table. "You can't really blame her for her reaction. It takes some getting used to."

Martin's head spun and he glared at his brother, then he shot up and marched down the hall to his bedroom. The door slammed as Kris sat back and stared at the kitchen ceiling.

* * *

A week passed. Kris worked hard on the house.
Martin became a recluse, leaving his room only for food
and to go to the toilet. The summer heat wave
continued. One day, dark clouds rolled across the sky.
Kris watched them approach and scooted indoors as the
rain began. It was slow at first. A drip as the wind
picked up and the sky darkened. Then the bottom fell
out and it poured. A prairie thunderstorm. Kris was
thankful he finished the roof. At least they would be
dry.

As the rain pelted the house, Kris walked to
Martin's room and thumped lightly on the door. "I'm
going over to Aunt Peggy Jane's," he said, pausing for
a reply. None came. Fuck it, he thought, sauntering to
the front door. Why the hell should he make the effort.
If his brother wanted to cut himself off from the world,
let him. He grabbed his blue wind breaker and walked
out. The rain struck painful blows. The car was only
twenty feet from the stairs but by the time Kris grabbed
the door handle and hopped in, he was soaked through.
The nylon shell was of little use in a thunderstorm. The
sky rumbled, but the green car rumbled louder as Kris
drove onto the dirt road which was transforming into a
river of mud. At times the rain was so heavy he couldn't
see through the car's windshield. Trees along the road
were bent to the ground by the wind. Three times Kris
narrowly escaped the ditch, the car fish-tailing blindly.
He let out a sigh when he pulled up beside Aunt Peggy

Jane's.

"Hello," Ruby chirped as Kris gave her a hug. He stepped from the living room into the kitchen where Aunt Peggy Jane was making bannock.

"How is she?" he asked.

Aunt Peggy Jane kneaded dough violently. "She's fine, but she hasn't once talked about Martin. Hasn't even mentioned his name." She flipped the dough and kneaded the other side. "How's he?" Aunt Peggy Jane asked.

Martin shrugged. "Quiet, he never comes out of his room, never talks, never does anything. I know he's hurting. Mom's reaction made him feel pretty bad, but he won't talk. I can't get near him." He turned to the window, watching hailstones slap to the ground as the storm worsened. "He takes lot's of pills."

"He has to," Aunt Peggy Jane said, pausing to look thoughtfully out the window. "I've been reading up on this sickness he's got. What a horrible way to die. I've been leavin' the magazines and newspapers around hoping your mother'd read them, but she won't."

Kris wondered at his mother's motives. Was it disgust over the lifestyle she never knew her youngest son led, or was it a defense from the shock and sorrow of his approaching death? He sensed some kind of personal battle was raging behind his mother's vacant eyes. Had she recovered enough to see it through?

"She's struggling with it," Aunt Peggy Jane said, reading his mind. "She's almost healthy, but she still has to learn how to cope with grief. It's destroyed her before and she's afraid."

"But she has to work it through before she can offer any compassion," Kris said, continuing the thought. "Martin has cried for her all his life. I hope to God she can answer him before he goes. Besides seeing the house completed, it's all he wants."

Aunt Peggy Jane nodded with remorse. She sighed, then rose and walked to the stove. "Want some tea?"

*　*　*

The sun shone and for a moment the humidity was high. Kris dodged giant puddles as he drove back to the house. Two rainbows stretched out across the sky, beginning at one corner of the reserve and ending at another. Even as an adult, Kris was fascinated by rainbows, as he was by the northern lights, lightning, and the eclipse he watched in 1979. He had an urge to race to the end of the rainbow and see what was there. Perhaps a pot of gold, perhaps colors, perhaps rain. On he drove. The house seemed lifeless as he got out of the car. There was no sign or sound of movement. He walked up the stairs and inside. He looked about. The place was neat and tidy, as it had been for days, but there was no sign of his brother. Kris turned and walked down the hall, then thumped loudly on Martin's door. He paused to listen, but there was only silence. "Martin," he called, "are you in there?" He reached down and grabbed the door knob, then turned it. The door opened with a creak and Kris stepped inside. Martin was in his bed, a lump under his covers. Kris thought it crazy to be using blankets when it was so hot.

He walked closer to the bed. When he reached the edge of the bed, Martin let out a moan and rolled over. Kris stopped, his mouth agape. Martin was covered in sweat and shivering. He seemed to be thinner and there was a vacant, unfocused look in his eyes. Without his makeup he looked terrible. Martin lifted his head, trying to speak, but his strength faded and his head collapsed back onto the drenched pillow. Blindly Kris ran into his own room and tore the blankets off the bed, then ran outside and threw them into the back seat of the car. Without pausing for a breath he raced back inside to Martin's room.

"All right," Kris said, placing his arms under Martin's limp body. "Let's get you to a doctor." Kris lifted his brother easily, and that worried him. He walked down the stairs and placed Martin in the back of the car. He covered Martin up, then spun around to the driver's side, jumped in, cranked the motor, slapped it in gear, and pounded the floorboard.

* * *

"Hang on bro, I'll be right back," Kris assured, flinging himself out of the car and towards the clinic. The doors flung open, quite startling the receptionist and two waiting patients.

"Where's the doctor?" Kris demanded.

Moments later, Kris flung open the door of the car and he and the young doctor peered in. The doctor stared at Martin who was shaking and sweating in the back seat. "He needs treatment immediately," he confirmed, "but he can't get it here." He looked from Martin to Kris, his blue eyes showing concern and regret. "I can't accept him as a patient into the clinic."

Kris was aghast. It took a few seconds to find his tongue. "What the hell are you talking about?"

The doctor turned and looked at the clinic window. James Caribou was staring out. When Kris saw the old councillor he suddenly understood, but he turned back to the doctor. "Who controls this clinic?" he asked.

"The band council," the doctor stated.

Kris turned and looked across the open prairie, his head wavering in disbelief. "Our cousin is on the band council," he mused, turning to look at his sick brother.

The young doctor sighed sympathetically. "Take him to Regina, they won't accept him anywhere else."

Kris' disbelief turned to anger. With gritted teeth, he turned back to the window where James Caribou still watched, then spun and raced back into the car. With a roar, the car took off, rifling rocks and dust into the air. "We're going for a drive," Kris said, his hands gripping the steering wheel tightly.

* * *

Kris hated hospitals, and Regina General was no different. Though small in comparison to Toronto's Mount Sanai, it had the same sterile environment and the same aura of sickness. He sat quietly staring at posters advocating health awareness and safety. Nurses strode by in neutral whites, patients in blue robes pushing IV stands. They shuffled to windows, staring out at the world like rats through cage bars. Beside Kris sat Dr. Mike Lewis, a specialist in infectious diseases. He had seen a few patients with Martin's condition, but knew the numbers would rise. His colleagues in Toronto had seen hundreds.

"Throw that list by me again," Kris requested. Dr. Lewis consulted Martin's file, not that he really had to.

"Kaposi's sarcoma, pneumocystis carinii pneumonia, and dysentery. It was the dysentery that nearly killed him."

"Is he out of danger?"

"No, the pneumonia still poses a strong threat. We're going to drain his lungs."

Kris looked away, feeling tears well up in his eyes. "What can I do?" he asked.

Dr. Lewis closed Martin's file. "Your brother is experiencing a lot of physical pain. The tumours from the sarcoma are through his body and he has to move slowly. He's also frustrated and angry, that's normal. Being his brother, a lot of his frustration might be vented towards you. It won't be easy, but just being with him will help."

"Does he have to be so isolated? He's being treated like he's radioactive."

"That's hospital policy," Dr. Lewis said, apologetically. He stood up and Kris joined him to walk down the hall. When Kris entered Martin's room, labelled and segregated from other patients, a nurse, wearing a mask with her hands wrapped tightly in sterile plastic, was leaving with a bed pan. Tubes and monitors were stuck to various parts of Martin's body. Kris smiled.

"Your own room," he said.

Martin looked up at his brother and for the first time since their mother showed up, Martin smiled, revealing a sarcoma lesion on the gum above his incisors. They're like icebergs, Kris thought, remembering Dr. Lewis' explanation. Martin had lost a lot of weight because it was too painful to chew.

"They're gonna fill my lungs up, then drain them," Martin said. "Gross eh?"

"You'll get through it. Dr. Lewis said they're gonna try a new drug on you."

Martin nodded. "My white blood count is too low for AZT and they won't give it to you unless you've made it through pneumonia. I guess they gotta try something. Did you tell mom?"

"Not yet. I haven't even found a place to stay."

"I have a friend, if you don't mind staying with him."

Kris smiled. "Why would I?"

They laughed until Martin started coughing, a hoarse, painful cough that made Kris cringe. "Kris," Martin said when the coughing subsided, "make sure they bury me on the reserve." For a moment, Kris wanted to crack a joke to lighten the mood, but decided against it. "I mean it, I want to be buried on the reserve," Martin insisted.

"I'll make sure," Kris said.

* * *

Martin's lungs were drained and he slowly recovered. Kris watched and waited, stricken with boredom, Saskatchewan boredom. The heat relented as August set in and the nights became cool. As Martin's recovery continued, Kris returned to the reserve and continued work on the house.

It was the same as he left it, unfinished. The weather had stained the unpainted wood, but everything else seemed fine. The roof was finished, the siding done, the walls insulated, and the dry wall half finished. There was still enough to keep him busy. The outside had to be painted and all the floors redone before the inside was painted. Kris smiled. After three idle weeks in Regina, there was finally something to do.

As he left the house for the band office, he reminded himself to finish the front steps. Without the bottom two rungs, someone could get seriously hurt.

It was a dusty day, dry and windy. Kris swore half the dirt in Saskatchewan flew around the band office. He stepped from the green car hoping to hold his breath until entering the office. When he glanced across the street at the Hudson's Bay store, the "downtown of the rez", he caught sight of Bev Pratt. As if feeling his stare, she looked up and saw him, then a dodge truck sped past along the road between them. The cloud of dust raised by the truck obscured Kris' vision. When it cleared, Bev was gone. Kris sighed, then turned to enter the band office.

"Frank Morris please," he told the receptionist. Grudgingly, she buzzed Frank over the phone.

Kris sat down and grabbed a copy of the band

newsletter. He thumbed through it, deciding to get his reimbursement check before confronting his cousin over the reserve clinic's sudden policy against Martin. The receptionist walked over.

"Can I have the receipts please?" she requested. Kris produced them and she walked away. Moments later, she returned with the cheque. "This is the last time we'll be able to cover your expenses," she explained. "We're having a cash flow problem right now."

Kris looked at her, suspicion in his breath, and asked, "Where's Frank?"

"In a meeting. He can't be disturbed."

Kris twitched his nose. Frank could at least have the decency to face him. He bolted up and started walking towards Frank's office.

"He's in a meeting," the secretary insisted.

"There's no fucking meeting," Kris growled. He entered Frank's office and slammed the door behind him.

"What the hell was that all about?" Frank demanded.

"What's all this about not being able to pay for any more repairs?" Kris demanded back.

"Look, I've stuck my neck out a long way already. It's against band procedure and it's costing a bundle. Right now, there isn't much cash available, and your house isn't a priority."

"Normally I'd believe you," Kris said, "but something smells, and it has to do with Martin."

"Martin?" Frank said. "What's he got to do with

it?"

"He was turned away by your clinic."

"Our clinic gets busy..."

"Fuck off! You and I both know why the clinic was told not to treat him. The same reason I won't get any more help to finish the house."

Frank paused a long time, then lit a cigarette. Deliberately, he exhaled the smoke in a tight, blue stream that floated and dispersed across the room.

"All right," he started. "The council found out about Martin when we received the clinic's report last month. Right away, they wanted him out. They're paranoid, Kris, they don't know a damn thing about the disease, but they don't want it on the reserve. I was outvoted nine to one, there was nothing I could do."

You could have said something, Kris thought. His suspicions proved correct, but that did nothing to quell the anger. In fact it grew. "I'm going to fight," he warned.

Frank nodded. "I thought you would, but remember, people are scared of this AIDS thing."

"I have a pretty good idea what I'm up against," Kris said, rising to leave.

"Kris," Frank said. Kris turned at the opened door. "You know where to find me if you need me."

"What I need is to finish that house before Martin dies."

Frank bit his lower lip. "I can't guarantee a damn thing, but keep the receipts, just in case."

Kris nodded, then left. Frank took another draw on his cigarette, exhaled and sat back with his tongue rolled firmly in his cheek.

* * *

Kris stepped into the dusty air. Squinting, he peered about, wondering what he was going to do. To fight was one thing; to know how, another. He hopped into the car and spun impatiently out of the parking lot. Maybe he could get a petition, but how many people on the reserve would really support him and Martin? His own mother wouldn't. Maybe a court order? He slammed the brakes and the car slid in the gravel to a halt. He checked the rear view mirror. Walking alone along the side of the road was Bev Pratt. He stepped out and confronted her. Bev stopped, staring hesitantly.

* * *

She'd been living in Vancouver, had a job as a secretary in a law firm. Married once, divorced, no children.

"No children?" Kris asked, sitting across from her in a Bonedry coffee shop.

"No children," she repeated in a way which indicated the question was closed. The conversation moved on. She'd attended university for a while, but dropped out. Went on to a business college and graduated. Held a job at the band office until her dad was voted out as chief. The new chief fired her and hired his niece. She let it go and left the reserve.

He recounted his past. Left the reserve for good

after their summer together years before. Held a series of menial jobs, none lasting more than three months. Got into school, fine arts, but quit. Too much drinking. Started painting a lot when not looking for work. Finally took to selling his paintings on the street. Got busted for canvassing twice, but kept going, then was offered a job at an advertising firm. He'd been there ever since.

"What brings you back?" she asked.

"Martin. He wanted to move back and asked for help in fixing up the old house. You?"

"I needed a break." Again her tone closed the issue. He noticed something different about her. A sadness. Maybe she saw too much in Vancouver, maybe she lived too much. Her looks hadn't suffered, that was for sure.

"I should be going," she said.

"Want a ride?"

The green gas guzzler was loud, too loud for decent talk. "Here," she yelled two miles past the band office. Kris pulled over. She opened her door.

"Can I see you again?"

She sighed. "It's been a long time."

"I remember it like yesterday."

"So do I," she said, closing the door.

There is definitely something different about her, Kris thought, watching her walk into her father's house. A large house built when he was chief, but run down because he hadn't held power in years. Perhaps if she would let him take her out he could find out what. Next time he ran into her, he'd have to pour on the charm. He laughed at himself, whatever charm he could muster would have to do. The laugh waned as his thoughts turned to Martin. He cranked the car into gear and drove off.

* * *

Over tea, Kris explained Martin's predicament to his mom and his aunt.

"Can you help me?" he asked.

Aunt Peggy Jane sat back and thought hard, her forehead forming a dozen wrinkles and her lips meshing together. Ruby's lips were tight, her eyes cold. "Whatever has happened to Martin is his own doing. It's his comeuppance for the way he's lived," she blurted.

Kris couldn't believe it. "He's your son for Christ's sake," he said, "and he's going to die. Can't he do it in dignity?"

Ruby didn't respond, neither of them did, but Ruby's face remained stone-like. Aunt Peggy Jane's was softer, but still unyielding. They both stared out the window. Kris stood up in a fluster. "Fuck you then, both of you," he shouted angrily. He stomped out of the house, slamming the door.

When she heard the car roar off, Aunt Peggy Jane turned to her sister. "Martin is still your son," she said in Cree.

Ruby said nothing, remaining defiant.

* * *

"I want to go home," Martin cried a third time. "I don't care how hard it's going to be. That's where I want to go and that's where I will go."

Dr. Lewis sighed. "It will be impossible to take care of you. You need daily attention and there's nothing on the reserve, and no one, to do it for you."

Kris sighed. "They won't take him," he stated flatly.

The doctor looked away and Martin said, "I've thought it over and I want to go home."

Kris sighed again. Martin had always been stubborn. He looked a lot better. He was still thin, but not skin and bones as when Kris brought him to Regina. His complexion seemed a lot healthier too, though Kris knew ninety percent of that was makeup. As for pain, Martin tried desperately not to show it. Painkillers helped. "All right," Kris conceded. "Get packed."

* * *

The green guzzler roared along the asphalt highway out of Regina, barely making it up the north side of the Qu'Appelle Valley. "I was wondering," Kris began, turning his eyes from the road. "Didn't you get any support from the gay community?"

Martin was quiet for a moment. Kris took the time to stare out across the amber prairie and its fields of grain. Already, the signs of harvest were on. Kris shook his head. There's no damn way he'd ever be a farmer. He had more security selling his paintings on Bloor and Spadina.

"They offer counselling, a buddy system and all that. Many are sincerely helpful," Martin said. "But for the most part, you're not really accepted unless you pretend you're something else. Being gay is one thing, being Indian and gay is another."

They left it at that.

Kris felt confident enough to take the back roads coming out of the valley. On a map, Saskatchewan has very few main highways, but the province is criss-crossed with thousands of dirt roads. When he hit an open stretch, Kris turned and watched his brother doze off with a smirk on his face. An extra dose of painkillers. It took two hours before Kris conceded they were lost. Frustrated, he parked the car and watched the sun dip out of sight. Pink and red shades filled the sky, bouncing off clouds. Nothing compares to a prairie sunset, he thought. There came grunts before Martin stuck his head up from the back seat. He looked around and then groaned, knowing they were lost.

"I suppose we're out of gas too?" he asked. And looked away before Kris could confirm this. Martin got out, then walked slowly around to the other side of the car and sat in the passenger seat. Slouched down, he propped his arm up on the window. "So now what?"

In the distance, they spotted an old, abandoned barn. They walked toward it. The smell withstood time, but the wood didn't. Kris entered, worried the walls might collapse on him. There was hay and straw, now coloured deep grey, lying everywhere. The stale smell was acute and Kris plugged his nose. It grew darker by the minute and Kris had trouble seeing as he worked his way towards the back of the barn. He walked into an old pickup with a thud.

Martin followed him into the barn. "Kris?" he called through the darkness.

"Over here," Kris answered. Martin walked up and sat down beside his brother against the old pickup's fender.

"Dad used to have a truck like this, didn't he?" Martin asked, squinting in the dark. He turned to look about the decaying barn as night settled its blanket. "It's eerie. Sort of like the house when we first started on it."

"Everything has a past," Kris said. "And the past haunts."

Martin nodded silently.

In the stable they found an old rubber hose and a bucket, then set about the task of siphoning gas from the pickup. Kris snapped his mouth away from the hose and let the fluid pour into the bucket. When they were sure the truck was bled dry, they left the dark barn and walked toward the car. The stars and the moon lit their way.

For a time they walked, both staring at the night's brilliance. Then Martin broke the silence.

"What haunts you out of your past?" he asked.

Kris let out a long, deep breath. "Bev Pratt," he said. He recounted the event from years before, from the night of the conception to the news of the doctor. "I really loved her," he said, "but I didn't want to end up like so many of the others. Always broke, unhappy, kids clawing for attention they'd never get. I didn't want any part of it." As he spoke, the confusion hung in his words like it had filled his mind. "So I ran."

Martin stared at the ground like his brother, sympathetic to Kris' shame.

"So you have a kid somewhere out there," Martin said, gesturing towards the horizon.

"No," Kris said, admitting the irony in his cowardice. "Bev had a miscarriage."

Martin whistled.

They poured the gas into the car and drove off. It was enough to get them to Lestock where they filled up and headed home. The reserve was quiet, the homes dark and dormant. Wearily, the brothers drove round a bend and turned into their driveway.

"The house is nearly finished," Kris said, as the head lights shone against their home. "Just needs to be painted." When the house came into full view, Kris slammed on the brakes. They jerked forward and back, then stared. Spray painted across the entire front of the house in green and silver were the words, FAGS GO HOME.

Kris turned off the lights and killed the motor. In the moonlight, he could still read the words. Martin got out of the car and walked towards the house. Kris followed.

"Where's the paint?" Martin asked. Kris pursed his lips towards the kitchen. They grabbed a can of paint and a brush each, then returned to the night. Silently, the brothers painted as the moon worked its way across the sky.

* * *

Kris and Martin worked hard on the house, scrubbing the interior, sanding walls and floors, installing electric outlets, and fitting in a wood burning stove. Martin never ventured out, and Kris only to buy materials, food, and beer. Each trip he doled out money and watched his bank account dwindle. Three times he'd returned to the band office seeking more money, and each time Frank said, "Funds are low right now."

Kris would try again the following week, and Frank's excuse would repeat itself. Finally, Kris showed up and said, "I'm flat broke."

"I wish I could help you," Frank said.

Kris returned to the house seething, and again Martin calmed him down.

"When they realize we're not going away, things will change," Martin predicted.

"I've got no more money," Kris stated. "We have no more food."

"We've got what we need to finish the house," Martin replied. "And enough food to last a few more days."

Grimy from varnishing wood, Kris spread the last bit of lard on the last slice of bread when he heard a car pull up and stop in front of the house. He and Martin went to the door and found Aunt Peggy Jane stepping out of Frank's Bronco with three bags of groceries. She thrust them into her nephews' arms and muttered something about not telling their mother.

The reserve took note of the brothers' progress, and

when the house was finished, word spread. Kris and Martin sat out front and made a toast.

"It's just like I remember it," Martin said, running his hand across his chin. "It feels like home."

"Still gotta fix those stairs," Kris said.

A car sped by on the main road. A head stuck out and shouted obscenities. Neither brother flinched.

The September wind blew, and with it flew leaves and dust. The butterflies were gone, replaced by seedlings. From the distance came a shotgun blast, followed by more as ducks scattered. Several flew over Kris and Martin.

"You can leave now if you like," Martin said. "I imagine your girlfriend is getting anxious."

Kris hadn't talked to Karina in weeks. During their last phone call he told her he didn't know when he'd be back. She told him to stay as long as necessary. For reasons not even clear to himself, Kris felt it was still necessary.

"Now that the house is fixed, what are you going to do?" Kris asked.

Martin shrugged, the prairie wind blew, and the brothers sat.

* * *

"Kris?" Martin said as his brother loaded firewood into the stove a week later.

"What?"

"I need my prescriptions refilled."

Kris turned to his brother. For the first time since they returned to the reserve, Kris saw a hint of fear in

Martin's eyes. He slapped the remaining log into the fire and stood up with conviction. "Come on little brother, we're going into town."

Like dogs in a circus, Kris and Martin stepped out of the car and into scrutiny. They had parked the large, green car off to the side of the clinic parking lot, but were still noticed. People stared and muttered hushed whispers, but defiantly the brothers strode forward and entered the reserve clinic. The blue-eyed doctor was gone. In his place they found an aging German with thick glasses. The young receptionist looked as Kris and Martin walked up. Kris threw the prescription on her desk.

"Can we get this filled please," he said, his voice a growl.

The receptionist was intimidated. Her head darted about in panic, searching for the doctor, searching for direction. The doctor walked forward. "I'm sorry," he stated. "This facility is not designed to care for people like you."

"All we want," Kris repeated in a restrained voice, "is to have this prescription filled." He pointed to it with one finger. The doctor looked at it, too.

"We don't carry any of the drugs you need," he said, staring through his thick glasses stubbornly.

"Could you read it to make sure."

"That wouldn't make any difference."

While they spoke, the reception area began to fill up as people entered the building. A small circle formed about Kris and the doctor. Martin had a front row seat. Kris snatched the prescription off the receptionist's desk and thrust it into the doctor's eyes.

"Read the fucking list," he growled.

Nonchalantly, the doctor's eyes focused on the piece of paper. Then he returned his stare to Kris. "Like I said, all those drugs are unavailable."

"When might they be available?"

"I can't say."

"Try."

The doctor, confident the large number of people in the building would back him up, suddenly grew bold. "When you and your brother are off the reserve."

Kris' face twisted as he drew his fist back. "No," Martin screamed, lunging forward. "Don't do it Kris," he said in a grinding whisper. He was holding Kris back, one arm firmly gripped on him. "It isn't worth it, none of this is worth it. We'll go back to Regina."

"Follow your brother's advice," the doctor said, "go back to Regina."

In the parking lot, Martin's walk was laboured. The exertion of holding Kris back put stress on his tumours, and he was wincing in severe pain. Kris tried to help.

"Are you all right?" he asked, grabbing his brother around the waist. Beneath the skin above Martin's hip was a large sarcoma tumour. Kris' left hand came down firmly upon it. Martin shrunk away in pain and fell to the ground, crying out. Several onlookers stared but no one offered to help. Martin remained on the ground, his body trembling.

"Martin?" Kris asked, uncertain of what he should do.

Martin let out a loud, gut-wrenching cry of

frustration. Kris stepped back. When Martin sat up, his face was filled with tears of fury. "I can't help what I've got," he yelled. "I don't want to die of this, but I can't do anything about it. I just want to die in peace, to die at home. Is that too much to ask for? Can't you let me do that?" A throng of people were gathered. Most spilling over from the band hall and the Hudson's Bay. All were quiet. Martin was staring up. No one knew if he was addressing them or God. "Can't I die in dignity?" he cried, his voice trailing off as his head fell. He sobbed. The crowd stirred. Something about open emotion made everyone uncomfortable. Kris was still, embarrassed, and embarrassed for being so. He wanted to reach out and hold his brother in his arms, but he hadn't done so since ... he didn't want to remember. He wanted to go to Martin and hold him, but he couldn't, and he didn't know why.

A woman stepped forward with a blanket and wrapped it around Martin. Then she sat with him and held him. Kris was thankful. Someone on the reserve still had compassion, and to his shame, it wasn't him. After a moment the crowd began to disperse. Returning to their busy lives. The woman continued to hold Martin, and Kris continued to stand above them. Soon, they were alone in the parking lot. The woman looked up. It was Bev Pratt.

* * *

Kris sat by himself in the living room. His eyes were large, staring at the fire in the wood stove as it leapt through air vents. Minutes passed and he didn't move, not until he heard footsteps in the hall. He looked up as Bev walked in and sat across from him.

"He's asleep now," she said. "He was upset and sorry he caused a big scene."

Kris shook his head. "He shouldn't be sorry ... I should be sorry."

"He needs more painkillers, that's all he's really worried about."

Kris stood, still feeling shame and determined to make up for it somehow. I can't just sit here, he thought, I have to do something. He grabbed his jacket and headed for the door.

"Where you going?" Bev asked.

"To find my cousin," Kris said with conviction.

At the door he felt Bev's arm on his. "I'll go with you," she said.

The roads were busy, which was dangerous, but it didn't matter to Kris. He sped along the dirt roads towards Frank's house. Bev, having found no seat belts in the green guzzler, held tight to the arm rest in the door as the car swerved about. Kris' lips were set tight. All he could think was that Frank was family, that he and Martin had counted on him. He spun the wheel to enter Frank's driveway and the car bounced heavily, the muffler scraping against the gravel, then skidded to a halt. Frank's Bronco wasn't in sight. He glanced up the hill to where Aunt Peggy Jane's house was. The Bronco wasn't there either. Kris jammed the stick into reverse and spun the car around, then gunned back onto the main road.

Frank would be at the bar. Kris glanced at Bev, but she stared straight ahead, holding onto the door tightly. They sped into Bonedry and spun into the hotel parking lot. Frank's Bronco was nowhere in sight. Kris parked, wondering what to do next.

"He's not here," he said. "Where the fuck can he be?" He wrenched open the car door and stood beside it in a fury, clenched fists at his hips. He looked blankly at the blinking neon sign over the hotel door. BONEDRY, it read in blue letters. Kris looked about. He kicked the ground and then got back into the car, slamming the door.

"In the state you're in," Bev said, "it's best that you don't find him." She put one hand on his arm, then withdrew it suddenly when he turned to her.

Kris sighed, knowing she was right. "Want a ride home now?"

She smiled. It was the same beautiful smile he remembered from years before. "Please," she said.

He cranked the wheel and they left town.

"I think I know what you're going through," she said, as the car bumped and roared through the night. "And I really admire you for it."

Kris pulled the car up in front of her father's house and parked. "He's my brother," he said, flatly.

"Yes, but there's more to it than that. You're feeling everything he is. I know you."

There was something in the way she said, 'I know you,' that made Kris turn and face her. She looked back at him. It was still the same, that look she had, and the way it reached him. He leaned forward a bit, searching for a response. She studied his face, seeking his eyes. There was longing in both of them. He leaned forward again, and so did she. It was like a time warp. Her lips just as soft, her embrace just as sensual. Her fingers glided tightly across his back, gently digging in, squeezing, probing. Kris felt the years melt away as he let go to their passion. Then she snapped away. Before he realized what was happening, she was going through the front door of her father's house.

* * *

It was a busy night at the Bonedry Hotel. The bar raked in a lot of money from the reserve. It always struck Kris as being unfair that white people of the town profited from a reserve's drinking problem, yet he played along willingly. Booze had that effect. Casually, he walked into the bar. A band was playing loud country music. Kris leaned against a pillar wishing he had money to at least buy a beer. He felt a light tap on his shoulder, and when he turned, he found James Caribou standing behind him. "I saw you and your brother tonight, at the clinic," James said. He drank twice from his glass before continuing, "And a couple of us got together and decided that it wasn't fair, what we were doing. Tomorrow, we're going to do something so he can get into the clinic and so that you get reimbursed for the house. I've driven by, you guys did a good job."

Kris didn't answer, but remained leaning against the pillar. He wasn't about to give thanks, and James

Caribou knew it. Taking another sip from his glass, James reached into his pocket and pulled out a fifty dollar bill.

"Take this," he said, pushing it towards Kris. Kris stared at it, but made no move. "Swallow your pride, I know you need it," James said. "Consider it part of your reimbursement."

Slowly, Kris reached out and took the money.

"I don't know if I should tell you this, but I will anyway," James said.

"What's that?"

"Your cousin Frank voted the same as everyone else. He didn't want you here either."

* * *

Drunk, Kris parked the car in front of the house and stumbled out. With deliberate steps, he walked towards the door. The moon was but a sliver and it was very dark. Kris remembered too late about the missing rungs on the front steps and he fell, his head colliding against the door with a thud. Groaning, he slid to the ground and stared up. The bright stars glittered and spun. Kris shut his eyes and battled an urge to puke. Why am I here, he thought. Then he remembered. Martin was dying. Martin, his little brother. Martin, whom he wouldn't hold after seeing what the priest at the boarding school did to him. It wasn't Martin's fault, Kris thought at the time. It was the priest. The faggy priest. What could Martin do? And yet Kris couldn't hold him, couldn't go near him. Martin had cried incessantly, and soon, Kris had too, but still, he couldn't go to him. Where was their mother? That's who Martin needed, but she had been in a hospital. Their dad was dead. Why was the Great Spirit putting them through this test? Why was the Great Spirit so mean? Kris thought only the white man's God was supposed to be mean. Kris couldn't hold Martin in his arms anymore. Martin had needed their mom, and their mom never came.

* * *

"He needs you, damn it," Kris seethed, his head throbbing from hangover and the bump he had from colliding with the front door. Ruby refused to answer. She stared straight ahead, pretending not to listen. "He's dying," Kris continued. "Doesn't that mean anything to you?" Still she refused to answer. "What the fuck is going on? Frank voted to have the clinic refuse Martin treatment and to quit paying us to fix up the house, and you still won't see him. What ever happened to family values? James Caribou talked to me last night. They're going to let the clinic treat Martin now and they will reimburse us, and he's not even family. Where the fuck was Frank with news like that?" He spun to confront Aunt Peggy Jane. "Frank, your son." The two women remained silent. Kris threw his arms in the air. "Then this family stuff must be bullshit, that's all I can see spewing all over this fuckin' reserve, bullshit. All Martin wants to do is die at home. You guys won't even give him that." He stood and walked to the door. He stopped and looked at Aunt Peggy Jane, "Thanks for the groceries." And he was gone.

Ruby stared out into the prairie, remembering her husband and her three sons as young boys, Ralph, Kris, and Martin. A family, she thought, trying to remember what it felt like.

*　*　*

Kris stormed into the clinic and walked past the startled young receptionist. He swung open a door and confronted the doctor. The doctor spun, his eyes wide beneath his thick glasses. Kris threw the prescription on the desk.

"Fill this out," he said.

The doctor grabbed the paper and read it. Begrudgingly, he stood up and walked into the back. He returned with several bottles of antibiotics and painkillers and dropped them in front of Kris. Kris scooped them into his pocket. Then looked into the doctor's eyes.

The doctor stared blankly as Kris walked out.

Kris made another trip to the band office, then to the bank in Bonedry before returning to the house. Martin was waiting eagerly on the front steps, almost doubled over in pain. Kris handed him the painkillers and Martin popped open the bottle and swallowed. Kris patted him on the shoulder, then watched as Martin entered the house. He seemed under control again. Kris sat on the steps and breathed a sigh of relief. All that was left was for Martin to die. Kris cringed at the thought, but that's exactly what it was. He wondered if it was still necessary for him to stay. He stood up feeling depressed.

"I'm going into town," he shouted as he walked towards the car. The car roared and sped off.

Martin watched out the front window. He shook his head and lay back down on the couch. His brother had done a lot for him, but he worried about Kris' drinking. Then an odd thought struck him. He was dying, yet he was worried about Kris. Kris who was healthy and took it for granted. The frustration bubbled in Martin as his fists clenched. Why me, he thought, why me?

The painkillers worked fast and soon Martin was asleep. His fists were still clenched.

* * *

Kris stood near the door of the Bonedry Hotel, drunk and wavering. Standing in front of him was a sober Bev Pratt. "How come," he slurred, spittle dripping from his lips, "you don't want me no more? Don't you find me attractive." His eyes lit up in an absurd show of affection.

"Go home," she said, her face a mixture of pity and disgust.

Kris shrugged and staggered out the door. In the parking lot, he fumbled with his keys, then somehow managed to open the car door and get in. He started the engine and it roared louder than necessary. He saw Bev standing outside the hotel and he rolled down his window

"Want a ride home?" he asked. Bev's eyes were sad as she shook her head. Kris shrugged again. "Friends don't let friends drink and drive," he slurred. Shivering, he rolled the window back up, then slammed the gas pedal and roared off.

At the house the car skidded to a halt as Kris' head thumped lightly against the windshield. He collapsed back into the seat, then shook his head, trying to clear fuzziness. He opened the door and started walking towards the house. Remembering the previous night's accident, Kris prepared himself for the stairs. But he stumbled over something and fell before he got there.

Stunned, he sat up, and fumbling in the darkness, felt along the ground. He found a foot. Squinting hard, he studied the face.

"Martin," he said, a distressed whisper. Close to hysteria, he shook his brother's limp body, but Martin remained a rag in his arms. Kris sat back, looking into his brother's battered face, blood from his nose and mouth caked against his skin. His shirt was torn, revealing welts and bruises from the beating. Struggling, he lifted Martin in his arms and carried him to the car. Tears streamed down Kris' face as he propped his brother up in the back seat. "Don't die Martin," he pleaded. "Not yet."

* * *

The night was without the moon, a time of month Aunt Peggy Jane had always disliked. She sat with Ruby in the kitchen smoking cigarettes and making earrings out of beads and quills. The table was cluttered with jars of beads, ashtrays, spools of thread, and two glasses of water containing two sets of false teeth. Over for a visit, Frank sat in the living room watching television. All was peaceful until they heard a roar, then a loud crash.

"What was that?" Ruby asked in Cree.

Before Aunt Peggy Jane could answer, they both heard a hysterical cry, "Mom!" At the door, standing in the light of the front steps was Kris holding Martin in his arms.

"He's drunk," Ruby muttered.

"Look at the other one," Aunt Peggy Jane scolded. In a moment she was rushing down the steps. She ripped a large piece of cloth off her dress and carefully mopped the blood on Martin's face. "Frankie," she yelled. Frank's head snapped when he heard his name. "Kris can't drive and this boy has to go to the hospital." When Frank didn't move, Aunt Peggy Jane stood and glowered at her son. "You take him to Regina," she commanded.

Swerving past the green guzzler crushed against the garage Frank drove off into the moonless night. Aunt Peggy stood in front of her house looking into the night. The bush, slightly lit by the porch light, hid the blackness beyond where Martin's car rested quietly, leaves already accumulating on its rusted surface. She turned and walked up the stairs and into the house, leaving Ruby alone with the night and the darkness.

* * *

Kris sat in the third floor waiting room slumped heavily in a chair. Had others been in the room, they might have thought him a patient, or that he should have been. His eyes were crimson, the circles beneath, black, his hair dishevelled. He was a mess, his appearance having changed little from the night before when attendants tried to admit him. A small television sat in the corner of the room. Kris stared blankly at the screen. It was a game show. A middle-aged man with a crew cut won ten thousand dollars and began jumping like a lunatic. Kris grabbed the remote and scanned channels. He settled on Sesame Street. Big Bird was chatting with a hairy mammoth, but Kris didn't get to see what happened because Dr. Lewis walked into the room. He spoke in a mechanical way about Martin's injuries, "Three broken ribs, hairline fracture on the jaw, broken nose, contusions covering much of his body," he listed. "But none of that worries me."

Kris cleared his throat, waiting. Dr. Lewis sat down beside him and closed his file folder. "Your brother's condition has deteriorated, not because of the beating, but because of the disease. His immune system has collapsed. Now he's developed anemia and his kidney's are failing."

Kris sighed as he leaned back against the couch. He closed his eyes, but he could still hear the doctor's words. "Your brother is going to die."

"How soon?"

"Soon," Dr. Lewis said, then added, "six to eight weeks."

* * *

Martin was quiet when Kris walked into the room on the ward set aside for terminal cancer patients. Kris sat down. The room was tubed. Tubes stuck out of Martin's body, out of the wall, from beneath the bed, and into machines. Surrounding the bed were machines monitoring Martin's pulse and respiratory rates. A bed pan sat under the bed and a box of surgical gloves were on the cupboard beside a sink. The sheets were white, hospital white. Covering Martin and the bed was a blue, wool blanket. Martin himself was blue. Welts and cuts covered his bandaged face and the sarcoma was clearly evident. It was the worst Kris had seen him.

Martin looked at him over the sheet. "I'm gonna stay in the hospital from now on," he whispered after several minutes. Kris' eyes shot up. He was about to object to Martin's decision, but thought of the pain they'd suffered on the reserve, the heartache, the antagonism, the embarrassment. "Anyway," Martin continued, "they won't let me leave." It's for the best, Kris thought, the reserve doesn't want us anyway.

It was late afternoon. Kris' hangover persisted. Martin drifted in and out of sleep. Still Kris sat in Martin's room leaving only when nurses changed Martin's catheter or attended some other bodily function. Then finally, the nurses quit asking him to leave. Kris stared out the room's window. Autumn was never more apparent. The sky was grey and drizzle fell. A tree's branches stretched by showing off its fall colours.

When Martin groaned or whined, Kris wanted to ask what hurt, but he knew it was pointless. Martin hurt everywhere. Later, Martin exhaled and relaxed. His eyes opened. Kris was able to produce a smile and Martin smiled back. "Make sure they bury me on the reserve, near dad and Ralph," Martin said.

Kris nodded. "I'll make sure."

Martin nodded. Later still he said, between lips which were quivering, "I'm scared."

Kris watched his brother cry, then stared out the window fighting his own tears. A fight he was losing. He turned to Martin and saw him staring straight ahead as the tears streamed down towards his ears. The eyes were squinted and his mouth was open in a quiet bawl.

Let it out, Kris thought angrily, the nuns won't hear. Tears spilled over and poured down Kris' face. He saw Martin as he was the night the nuns returned him from the priest's, crying, a frightened, lonely little boy. Martin needed to be soothed, to be loved, to be held. Hesitantly, Kris moved towards the bed and sat on its edge. Martin looked up, his eyes almost pleading. Kris shook, then reached out and wrapped his arms around Martin's shoulders. Martin's arms wrapped around Kris and he wept. Kris cleared his nose and throat.

"There was a snake," he began, "a green snake who lived in the slough. When it was dry, the snake stayed in the muddy wetness, but when it was wet, the snake would go for walks. Side to side it walked, wriggling like this."

And he wriggled his arm in the air to show how the

snake did it. Martin looked up to watch, then stared towards the door. Kris turned the same way. In the room, ahead of Frank and Aunt Peggy Jane, stood Ruby Morris.

Kris became quiet as Ruby stared at Martin, then she stepped forward. Kris moved away to make room for her on the bed and she sat down, running a hand affectionately across Martin's cheek. She grabbed his other hand and squeezed. Tentatively, Martin squeezed back. She lifted his hand to her mouth and kissed it, then lowered it to her bosom.

"The snake went for a walk," she began, grabbing the tissue to wipe Martin's eyes. Aunt Peggy Jane and Frank disappeared around the corner. Kris stood up and watched his mother continue the story. The tears still dripped and stained his eyes red, but he smiled as he left the room and wandered down the hall.

Outside, people were entering and leaving the hospital at a quick pace. Kris watched, wondering for a moment what their stories were, who they were visiting. Towards the street, trees stood tall on the boulevard. Cathedral-like, they stretched one by one on both sides down the street and out of sight. Kris noticed Frank's Bronco parked there. An officer was tucking a parking ticket under the front, left windshield wiper. In front of the truck stood a tall elm tree, its branches bare from dutch elm disease.

"Six to eight weeks," Kris mused quietly.

It took three.

* * *

Martin's wake was a boisterous affair, like all wakes on the reserve. What caught Kris off guard was that people came, in droves. Ruby and Aunt Peggy Jane cooked a feast and James Caribou told dirty jokes to old women, who giggled incessantly and flashed their gums. Serenely, Martin's body rested in the centre of the room. It was an expensive coffin, but Martin left behind enough money in his will to cover the expenses. He was buried on the reserve, right by his father.

Bev Pratt showed up about midnight.

"Quite a turnout," she commented as Kris met her by the door.

"Mom and Aunt Peggy Jane pulled it off," he explained. "But it was Martin who insisted we have it at the house. He figured we spent so much time fixing it up, we might as well use it." Bev looked the house over appreciatively. "You guys did a good job."

Kris shrugged.

"I know you're leaving soon," she said. "And I want to talk to you before you go." Bev motioned towards the door. They walked out into the night. The moon was haloed, and it was cold. Bev zipped up her jacket, Kris shivered. "Look," she said, "I remember what we had, and I remember that it was good, despite what happened at the end. It would have been so easy to start over. You were the first person I ever really loved. No matter who comes along after, the first one always remains."

Kris nodded his agreement.

"But I couldn't get into a relationship with you

again," she said.

Kris watched her with questioning eyes.

"Just before I left Vancouver," she continued, shifting her gaze to the haloed moon. "I tested HIV positive. I have the AIDS virus."

Kris looked to the ground. After a while he said, "Thanks for coming to Martin's wake."

Bev's eyes warmed. "You're welcome."

"So what are you going to do?"

Bev stopped walking and stared into the stars. "I don't have the full blown disease yet. But I think I'm going to stay here. Being with you and Martin really helped me put things into perspective. I can handle it now. And you?"

Kris thought out loud. "Go back to Toronto. Convince my boss to take me back, convince Karina to take me back, then carry on."

"Think you'll ever come back here?" Bev asked.

"Oh yeah, I'll come back."

"Will you visit me?"

"Of course I will."

"Don't make any promises you can't keep, Mr. Morris," Bev laughed.

Kris smiled. "You think you know me so well," he goaded.

"Because I do."

Kris laughed. "Want to go for a walk?"

"I don't know," she said, acting coy. "Guys like you mean trouble."

They laughed and walked towards the road. The wind blew dead leaves as winter's breath hummed about.

"Maybe they'll find a cure," Kris wondered.

"Maybe you'll quit drinking," Bev countered.

"Maybe."

About The Author

Of Cree, Ojibwe, Irish, English, Scottish, and French descent, Jordan Wheeler was born in Victoria in 1964. His roots are widespread, but he feels a closeness to the Touchwood Hills area of Saskatchewan. Perhaps one day he'll go there.

Jordan works in video, film, and popular theatre when he's not writing. He currently lives in Winnipeg with his family and cat.